High Hopes

By John M. Olsen

Three Ravens Publishing
Chickamauga, GA USA

Contents

Dedication:

To those who have risked or given their lives defending others.

And, as always, to Kelly.

Acknowledgments:

Writing in an already-defined universe comes with a mix of challenges and opportunities, and I want to thank the Three Ravens Publishing team for being so easy to work with. I have family and friends who have served in the military, but not being a veteran myself, it helped to have a pool of experts in the Three Ravens author community to draw upon as I navigated both historical combat and the existing lore and history of the JTF.

I also have to thank my friend Jay Barnson. While I was researching World War I biplanes, he mentioned he had a VR flight simulator. I spent way too much time flying around France in a virtual biplane. I discovered how hard it is to shoot a moving target with a moving gun. I also discovered the joys of VR-induced motion sickness.

Lastly, I must thank you, my readers. Without your support and reviews, my books would be nothing more than an occasional idea bouncing through my head. You inspire me to take "wouldn't it be cool if..." and turn it into published stories.

The Aerodrome

Reconnaissance via airplane could win the Great War, if only they could get the right people and equipment into the right places. It always came down to logistics.

Lance Corporal James Jackson, USMC, glanced at his watch, then off to the north horizon, where scattered clouds obscured a clear view. The makeshift airfield at the Le Bourget Aerodrome in northern France had served as his home for several months, always buzzing with the activity of people and biplanes. The mid-morning sun crept higher in the eastern sky, burning off the last remnants of morning mist. A light chill hung in the still summer air. Jackson checked his watch again. "Hey, Moreau, weren't they due back by now?"

His gunner and bombardier, Sous-Lieutenant Marcel Moreau, sat at a table nearby, assembling a new set of customized bombs, one of his specialties. "The time, it means nothing to them. They see something interesting, they stay longer."

Jackson took a deep breath and identified the smell of fuel drifting on the air, overpowering the smell of the runway's fresh-cut grass. "I hope that's it. They brought back fantastic pictures last time, and they have a big report due. Did you read their last debriefing? They found German troops where someone suspected some of the Kaiser's men might be gathering deeper into Belgium. Nobody on the ground could have possibly discovered them, so maybe now we can get a little more recognition for our work in the air. I can't wait to get out there to help map out this new grid myself."

The flights were dangerous, especially with many ground forces now equipped with guns designed to shoot down aircraft. The value of the information outweighed the danger, but an airplane could only stay in the air for so long before running out of fuel.

"Oui, I saw the debriefing, but I do not share your enthusiasm. When we end this war and fill the terrible trenches, I will be happy. You see what it is like. Death comes even without bullets." Moreau made the sign of the cross.

Jackson recalled the story Moreau had told one night when he'd had too many drinks under his belt. "There's nothing inspiring or noble about dying from infection in the trenches." Jackson pondered the green grass between his feet. "But that doesn't matter. Your brother is a hero for his service, plain and simple…as much as any soldier can be. It makes no difference how he died if it was for home and country. Your family should be proud of his time spent defending France."

"Thank you for your kind words."

Jackson knew others hadn't been so kind in their comments, so he lent moral support to his friend whenever he could. Returning to his worries over the late aircraft, Jackson said, "I still think it's foolish to send single planes out, even on night missions. Two can support each other. I don't care if we can hide in the dark and the clouds. Things go wrong. They always do, like when we ran into that anti-aircraft gunner and had to run from three triplanes all on the same flight. Definitely not flying that route again."

The new route taken by the late Farman MF.11 biplane should have been clear flying all the way into Belgium and back. The rugged terrain and lack of improved roads meant the enemy couldn't haul heavy equipment or set up artillery for a large swath of the targeted terrain. Roads became more frequent only near the airplane's maximum range, and that was where the other team's reports of enemy movement originated, deep within Belgium.

Simple missions held a strong appeal, and this one qualified: they were to use the moonless hours, after the waxing quarter moon set, to fly deep into enemy territory. They would confirm the rumors of enemy troop movements, get whatever counts and locations they could in the early morning light, and get back in one piece. All the information in the world wouldn't help if you didn't make it back to report on the trip. And now the fliers had vanished.

Moreau hefted another finned bomb into the wooden crate beside his assembly table, then brushed his hands off. "I have parts to build a larger bomb. Would you like to see?"

Anything was better than the tension of waiting for a late airplane and the two men it held. "Sure. What have you got?" Jackson straddled a chair and sat at the table as Moreau pulled the lid from a new box and retrieved steel parts one at a time like a proud parent.

"You see the payload for the bomb? It is larger."

That was the one part of Moreau's packages Jackson understood. The rest of the pieces were a jumble of wires, springs, fins, and buttons. But payload he understood. A bigger explosive compartment created bigger explosions. They hadn't done much active combat as a team, but he was all for taking out targets of opportunity as they flew through occupied Belgium on their almost-daily scouting runs. "I like it. How many of those things can you carry?"

Moreau scowled. "Parts arrived for only one. The rest are smaller, like before." He set the parts out and went to work with his tools as an armored car pulled to a stop nearby.

The driver got out, marched over to the table, and stood at attention. He and Moreau exchanged a few words in French, the driver's expression growing more frustrated as the conversation continued.

Jackson looked to Moreau with an eyebrow cocked, hoping to be filled in without having to ask for a translation. That was the biggest problem with his work as a trainer on loan to the French military. He spoke no French, which put him at the mercy of his flying partner for every conversation.

"The driver has come to pick up Lance Corporal Clark and Mr. Laurens, since they were to be here by now. He is not happy that I know nothing of their delay. Like us, he is stuck waiting." The French soldier returned to wait in his car. "You and Clark are both Americans. How long have you known him? Did you fly together before coming here?" asked Moreau.

"We're both assigned as trainers and observers, but I never met him until we ended up here together at the Aerodrome. The Marines picked us out and sent us because we both know how to fly an airplane. I suppose the French government asked for a little help. I'll never understand how all that works. Did you know Mr. Laurens before coming here?"

"Only by reputation. Rumors say he has been a part of the Belgian underground for quite some time, fighting against the German occupation. The man is also an observer like you, but he is not military."

A non-military observer. Jackson knew that was just another way of describing a spy. That sort of work was so far out of Jackson's specializations that the man always seemed a mystery. At least he was working for the good guys. "I don't even know his first name. I think he does that on purpose to seem mysterious or something. Mr. Laurens, the enigma. A shadowy figure cloaked in darkness."

Moreau continued to assemble the parts of his bomb as they watched the sky for signs of the missing airplane. "You may be right. He escaped Belgium after the occupation and had a trusted contact in France."

"Well, I'm glad to have him. He really knows the geography we've been flying over." Jackson dug out one of his earlier memories of Mr. Laurens. "I've worked with him in the office, and he's a great one to have around. I even flew with him a time or two, before you got here to take his place. The stoic and mysterious Mr. Laurens had me cracking up the first time we flew together. He was like a kid in a candy store, seeing all the sights from so high, pointing at the towns, the mountains, everything. He didn't even vomit his first time, which is always a bonus. I hate washing out the airplane."

The missing spy hadn't made many friends, so Jackson's exchange of information with Moreau dwindled as they ran out of gossip on the man. Mr. Laurens was a good man, and now he and his pilot were late. Not just late, but late for a planned meeting. That was serious. "Moreau, what do you say we go up for a look around to see if they're in sight? We can fly a half-hour out and back."

Moreau set his tools in a nearby toolbox, fitting each into a custom, velvet-lined spot. He wrapped his work-in-progress in a rag and laid the casing of the twenty-five-pound bomb gently into the box it had come from. "Later, my dear, we will get to know one another." He closed the lid and patted the box.

Jackson laughed. "You need a girlfriend. Tell the driver we'll go up to watch for them, and I'll meet you at the plane."

Within minutes, Jackson was in his element in his Avro 504, strapped in and accelerating along the field, Moreau buckled into the front seat with binoculars at the ready.

Jackson pulled on the stick, and they roared into the sky. The pressure forced him into his seat as he reveled in the feel of the responsive aircraft. A couple of wing waggles later, he began a spiral up to gain altitude as Moreau scanned to the north for the missing plane.

There was a chance the missing crew had become disoriented, but the later it got, the greater the chance something terrible had befallen them, taking them to the ground somewhere along their route. Unexpected anti-aircraft fire? A lucky German taking a shot with a rifle? Even ordinary engine trouble could strand them as much as a hundred miles behind enemy lines, with no way of sending a message back to the Aerodrome.

After an hour, Jackson spiraled back down and landed, fuming at their failure to see any sign of the missing plane.

He threw his goggles into the seat with disgust as he climbed out, taking his inability to spot the plane as a personal failure. "We have to go look for them. If the enemy shot them down, we need to know where those troops are. If other trouble found them, they may be out there with no way to get home, and no supplies."

Moreau nodded. "If we see them on the ground, we can send others to help."

Jackson recognized Moreau's subtle way of reminding him there was no way to land or pick up extra passengers, even if they managed to find them.

"Mr. Laurens knows his way around Belgium. They may be on their way back home on foot. I'll write up the request for a search mission and see what I can do." He knew how slim the chances were once an airplane vanished. Nobody bet on odds like that.

"We have two men missing, sir. I would like to understand your objections to the search." Jackson wanted to rant at Colonel Dubois, commander of the Aerodrome, as he stood at attention in front of the man's desk in the base office. The well-aged officer had come from Paris only two weeks prior, and the old soldier had yet to understand how to make good use of aircraft. He was a career Foreign Legion officer, more adept at ordering men on horseback than sending men to fly air support far above the ground troops he understood so well. The world was in a state of constant change, and the old guard didn't always see the value in change. Some actively fought against anything new.

"There is nothing to be done. This is war. We lose men. Dead, alive, they could be anywhere." At least the man had passable English, an important skill with the multi-national forces assembled by the growing Allied forces.

Someone had to do something to locate the missing men, and Jackson knew he was the most qualified pilot at the airfield. Moreau was the best spotter in the Aerodrome, as well, but that was only because the very best, Mr. Laurens, was out there somewhere, missing. Jackson's training came to the fore. He clamped his mouth shut before he said something he would regret later. Since insulting his temporary commanding officer would get him nowhere, he took a different approach.

"We also have their missing airplane to consider. It will be hard to replace, along with the weapons and cameras. They had a planned flight path that shows everywhere they might have stopped or been shot down. We may be able to recover some useful equipment from the crash site—and keep it out of enemy hands—even if the aircraft and the men have been lost."

Colonel Dubois rubbed his graying goatee in thought. *Bingo.* He was either concerned about the expensive matériel, or he knew enough about the new tools of warfare to value aerial photography. Jackson pushed his luck a little farther, adding in more justification. "We can fly the same path looking for them. That will also get us the critical information they were after to confirm troop movements."

"Tell me, what could be the cause? What could stop them? They can fly over everyone."

It would take too long to explain the mixed advantages and challenges of using military aircraft in warfare. He had to keep it simple for the old soldier, avoiding the delicate nature of the aircraft.

"The reason for them not coming back? There are several possibilities, sir. The enemy could have shot them down. Engine trouble would put them on the ground, but in one piece. There's a chance Mr. Laurens saw something he needed to put eyes on up close, but I consider that highly unlikely. They wouldn't land behind enemy lines unless it was the only option. The team wouldn't break protocol like that. It had to be equipment failure, either internal or caused by enemy forces."

It was hard to tell if he'd made any headway, but at least he hadn't been kicked out or grounded. Jackson waited for a few moments to allow Colonel Dubois to think it over.

Finally, the colonel leaned back in his chair and shook his head. "The risk is high."

Jackson felt the change in the old soldier's tone. Despite the rejection, was there a chance he could go out on the search after all? "We can fly out at sunup and enter Belgium along a lightly monitored section of the border with France. That's already part of the flight path, since we designed it that way. Searching by the light of day raises the chance of success. We fly back after searching their anticipated flight path. We go exactly where they planned to go, but in the daytime, so we can see if they're on the ground. Another option to reduce risk is to fly out at night and search in daylight on the way back, just like our recent reconnaissance missions. That will match what the missing airplane did, as we complete their original mission, but we can search for the missing men and airplane as well."

"No. A request has come in for help on the border. The new orders take precedence. The enemy builds a stockpile that must be destroyed. Once that mission is complete, you may resume the regular scout path taken by the other *avion*. We must meet our obligations to assist others, and then we will finish our work to map enemy movements. You may search then, but you may not deviate from your assigned routes and flight times."

The old cavalry colonel knew how to evaluate risk, and was at least willing to listen to new ideas, but it was clear he'd already marked off the missing team and airplane like a loss in a ledger. "Are you sure you won't allow us to fly the full mission run in daytime?"

"Was I not clear? You have flights to prepare for. Dismissed."

It wasn't a total defeat if the colonel would allow him to sweep the path on his way back, but the delay of the additional mission frustrated Jackson. He took his minor victory and held it tight. "Very well, sir. I will continue our scheduled flights after our trip to the front lines." And once he resumed the scouting and mapping missions, he would push the limits and search as much as fuel allowed.

The pilot and bombardier stood at a flimsy table as a team fueled their aircraft and prepared it for flight. A look of concern crossed the Frenchman's face. "Such a mess. We face ground fire from mobile gun placements, and we have reports of air patrols nearby. We don't even know what airstrip they fly from."

"I'll keep an eye out for the airplanes. I'm not so worried about the rest," said Jackson, with a very American grin. He pointed at a trench line more than forty kilometers away. "There'll be a heavy ground patrol cutting through just behind the trenches here, making a lot of noise to draw attention. I called in a favor. They're already in motion."

"Good. Enemy movements will cause weak points in the line we can fly through. I have worked with the ground troops near here. They are good at giving flag signals." Moreau waved at their proposed route where it crossed the front line, indicating the best routes into and out of the target area. Rather than the deep fortified trenches farther to the northwest, the area was more fluid, with a give and take of territory as troops ebbed and flowed in offensive and defensive moves. Jackson's requested ground patrol would look like just another possible incursion the enemy had to respond to.

Later, as they approached the area, Moreau signaled to keep it straight and level as they crossed over French troops. Jackson trusted Moreau's directions after surviving several dangerous missions together. The Sous-Lieutenant had saved both their lives more than once by avoiding or pointing out dangerous gun placements. The pilot scanned the horizon and the sky above for the rumored enemy aircraft, and found none, while Moreau monitored the ground for signals. It wouldn't do at all to be surprised by airborne enemies.

"Any word of gun placements to watch out for?" Jackson could dodge and weave with the best of them, but the best plan was not to get shot at in the first place.

Moreau shook his head. "We are clear for now. Here is the front line below us."

It might be easier than he'd planned if the enemy guns no longer guarded their flight path. He'd have to send a bottle of Scotch whisky to the patrol he'd arranged. It was nice to catch a bit of luck on their way to the enemy's forward weapons depot.

The Frenchman peered over the side toward the ground and pointed to indicate he'd located the target for their mission. He signaled for the pilot to perform a hard-left banking turn. Jackson rolled to the side and pulled up on the stick. The aircraft lost velocity in the turn, but Moreau soon signaled a straight course and pulled two of his bombs out from between his feet. He held one out to each side, leaning as far back as he could to avoid dropping them onto the lower wing of the airplane. Jackson had heard rumors of a bombardier who had done just that, landing a bomb on his own aircraft wing, blowing out the wooden supports. With no structural support, the wing had collapsed. The aircraft fell, killing both crewmen on impact. Moreau was much too careful for a novice mistake like that.

While Moreau had his task to worry about, Jackson had his own, keeping them safe from other aircraft. He scanned the sky to the front and the sides as his apprehension grew. Confidence in his own flying didn't mean he sought out trouble, and even a little lapse could get them shot down by either air or ground forces.

John M. Olsen

Out of simple paranoia, he turned and gave the sky a quick scan behind them and found nothing. Then straightening out, he leaned back to get a better view around the upper wing.

There—obscured during his first scan because of the aircraft wings—was a dark speck high at one o'clock. If it was a single plane, he had a good chance against it, but he'd rather complete their bombing run without getting shot at by another pilot. Over the engine noise, Jackson yelled, "We have company!"

Moreau signaled to hold straight and level, even as Jackson prepared for a dogfight. The longer he held their course, the more likely he'd engage with the other pilot. To complicate issues, Moreau was responsible for the machine gun mounted on the top wing above his head, and he couldn't shoot and drop bombs at the same time.

Jackson scanned to the sides as he tracked the enemy airplane to avoid being swarmed. Two specks appeared behind the first. Three-on-one didn't look good. Memories of his last encounter with three enemy aircraft flashed into his mind, sounding mental alarms that urged him to escape. He was good, but so were the Germans. "We've got two more. They're flying together in formation." If the new arrivals were older models, he could outrun them, but not until Moreau did his job and the mission objective was met. Moreau continued to signal straight and level as he peered over the edge of the plane's fuselage from his seat, struggling to get the view he required.

Moreau removed his restraints and leaned farther out. Great. If Jackson had to get creative with his flying, his gunner might fall out. He'd warned him about the trick before, but he never listened. Straight and level. Right toward the three enemy planes closing fast from the north.

Moreau switched to hold both bombs in one hand and pulled out a third, hanging all three over the left edge of the fuselage. He nodded his head at one-second intervals, a favorite timing trick Jackson had watched him perform several times on various missions.

He dropped two bombs, waited a moment, then dropped the third before giving a signal to do an Immelmann.

"Are you crazy? Your belt's not on!"

He repeated the signal as he fumbled with something at his feet.

Jackson mumbled, "You better know what you're doing, you crazy Frenchman." He pushed the throttle to full and dove to pick up speed before pulling the stick back to its stops.

The plane arced up and over as the blood rushed from his head at the force of the loop. A view of the ground spread out underneath him at the top of his half loop, just in time to see Moreau's first bombs explode to the front and rear of their target in a triple flare of light and smoke. He'd missed, doing little more than adding small craters in the roads running to and from the stockpile.

Before Jackson could roll upright, Moreau somehow stood and emptied the rest of his box by opening it and letting the small bombs rain downward in a flurry as he dangled upside down, his head held even with the top wing. He then tossed the box for good measure and grabbed hold of the wing with both hands as he defied gravity in his inverted position.

Jackson rolled the plane upright and left the throttle at full to outrun the approaching trio of enemy airplanes. They hadn't closed to reliable gun range, so escape was likely, unless they wanted to chase him back into French-controlled territory and brave fire from the ground. He certainly wasn't going to stick around to shoot at the airplanes when Moreau had no more bombs to drop.

A rumble erupted from below, much larger than the small bombs could produce on their own. The plane rattled from the shockwave of detonating explosives as the stockpile went up in a giant fireball. Moreau glanced over the side and to the rear. His face lit up as he let out a laugh of relief, then gave a double thumbs-up signal before clapping his hands together.

Glancing to the rear, Jackson saw the three specks in the sky spreading out as they gave up their attempt to catch him. They were almost close enough to identify the model as he got a good profile view. Likely triplanes with tighter maneuverability than his Avro 504K. He'd seen both biplanes and triplanes in the area on earlier missions. He made note of their approach and retreat path so the tactical folks could estimate the location of their home base.

Many of his flights into enemy territory were a game of sorts, a contest of skill with one pilot against another, carried out at long range. Fly into enemy air, make a nuisance of yourself, then fly out before the sparse air coverage could intercept you. The enemy did the same, working to strike where coverage was weak. Then the ground forces would adjust, and the game would play out all over again with forces in new places.

Jackson was done playing the game for today; it was time to get back over the line and head for home. The recon mission came next on the Aerodrome schedule, and there was much still to be done before that flight. Also, he had to decide whether to congratulate or reprimand Moreau for his antics on the bombing run.

The meeting room at the Aerodrome could hold over a dozen comfortably, but Jackson had invited only Moreau and Colonel Dubois.

The colonel started things off. "You succeeded, yes?"

Jackson nodded. "Yes, sir. We destroyed the target."

"Then why do we meet? You must prepare for a reconnaissance flight tonight. Is there more you must report?"

Jackson ran through the highlights in his head, but decided against giving the colonel any information that might be used against Moreau in the future. Reports to the colonel for the just-completed mission would only emphasize their success, since the results spoke for themselves. Rather than mention his flying companion's odd methods, he moved on to a more worrisome point.

"Three airplanes nearly intercepted us. We need to fly in groups for better defenses. We have a second plane available to go with us tonight, but we need your approval."

"Denied." The colonel hadn't even considered it as an option. "You will fly the mission as it was planned, and you will report what you find. The plan is already good enough. I want a report on troops and their movements. Keep to your regular return path and do not divert to search for the missing *avion*."

"I…yes, sir." Though this went against the colonel's earlier statement that we could search as we came back, it would do no good to point that out or to argue.

"Is there anything else you must tell me that is not in your reports?" Colonel Dubois stood, indicating he was done, whether Jackson had covered everything or not. The bite of the comment was not lost on him, and Jackson fumed inside, wondering if the colonel provoked him on purpose.

"No, sir. We will finish our preparations for the mission."

Jackson worked to unclench his jaw and relax through a series of deep breaths. The anger faded into the background where he could manage it. He pulled the door shut behind himself as he left the Colonel's office. Then his curiosity got the best of him, and he turned to Moreau with the eagerness of a schoolboy to ask, "How did you pull off that stunt in the plane without falling out?"

John M. Olsen

Moreau said, "I tied my boot laces to the seat. I could not fall. It is too hard to see everywhere from sitting."

"Warn me next time, would you?"

"But now, you see, you already know. I prepare before I act. Trust me."

"Trust? But your first bombs missed. I thought you were a better aim than that."

"Ah, but did you not see? The roads in and out were first, then the depot. They did little damage, but kept everyone at the depot, unsure which escape was safe. With your excellent flying, we succeeded." He made the sound of an explosion and waved his arms with a grin, simulating the detonation of the ammunition depot. The man enjoyed his job.

Jackson filed his paper reports and headed out to make sure the plane had a full load of fuel and ammunition while Moreau resupplied on bombs. At the arms depot, the two men loaded a crate onto a cart, then a nearby Frenchman helped push the cart out to where the airplane sat tethered to the ground. The men were used to the drill and needed no instructions; they passed belts of ammunition up to Jackson as he loaded them into the airplane and ran them through the feed mechanism to the gun.

Topping off the tanks with fuel was simpler, even if the fuel cans weighed more than the ammunition. Soon, his tasks were complete, and Jackson did a quick inspection out of habit, looking over the painted canvas airframe and the control wires. All was in order, yet a sense of foreboding grew in his mind. He shook his head. It did no good to speculate on the cause of the airplane's disappearance without more evidence.

With his inspection complete, Jackson headed to his bunk to catch whatever sleep he could before takeoff in the middle of the night. Catching half a night of sleep would feel like a luxury compared to some recent night missions he'd flown.

The trip over Belgium held little excitement, but the nighttime views were beautiful in their own way. The moon had set during the flight, no longer bathing the countryside in its ethereal white glow. Jackson found the twinkling lights of a landmark town in the dark, adjusted his heading, and moved on to the next. It was Moreau's job to note any glimmer of habitation not already on their maps, since it could be troops from the Central Powers, most likely occupiers from the Kaiser's forces. Camps were terrible at blackouts. Someone always forgot a campfire or figured the tent would hide their lantern instead of making the whole tent glow when viewed from above.

On the next segment of the path, the terrain was devoid of lights for miles. While much of Europe had good roads and frequent towns, this mountainous area felt isolated and primitive with its dark forests and lack of human intrusion. Jackson imagined what it might be like on the ground with no sign of civilization nearby, except for one lone airplane buzzing high above.

The hairs stood up on the back of Jackson's neck, making him second-guess his every move. Was he on the right course? He checked his compass with a tiny electric lamp he'd wired into the cockpit for night missions. He sighed in relief, feeling foolish about jumping at shadows in the dark. Night missions like this one had been part of his routine for months, yet something felt different tonight.

To ease his sense of paranoia, he climbed five hundred feet higher, and then reduced his throttle to the minimum for a chance to listen for enemy gunfire or engines. Nothing. He set the throttle back to normal to maximize his range.

Like a shadow against the darkness, something flickered in Jackson's peripheral vision and was gone. Leaning forward, he yelled, "Keep an eye out. Something doesn't feel right." Had it been just a trick of his eyes? He adjusted the fit of his goggles, making sure they were snug. Jackson knew better than to disregard his subconscious promptings to pay attention to his surroundings.

"Oui. The darkness, it oppresses me as well." Moreau went through the motions of verifying the machine gun feed, letting his nerves show as he alternated between adjusting the gun and scanning the night sky.

The glint of two red flecks of light caught Jackson's attention off to his left, then it was gone again. Just as he prepared to disregard it as nothing, Moreau pointed and said, "Gauche. Left. There was a red light."

They weren't alone in the sky. His plane was as invisible as the enemy's plane in the moonless night. He had to rely on the darkness to cloak his location, but he could do nothing about the sound of his engine. Jackson adjusted his heading by a few degrees as a precaution to throw off anyone who might have seen him, then idled the engine once again. No noise reached him from beyond his own aircraft. It was little consolation, given the short distance between him and anything he could hear, but every bit of advantage helped.

The plane rocked as the tail dropped from an impact, prodding a yelp from Jackson as he slammed the throttle to full and banked. "What was that? Did you see it?" With the roar of the engine, Moreau couldn't hear his yell. He scanned the sky above and saw nothing. No dark shape drifting across the star-speckled sky. With no moon, the only way to spot something was to see when it obscured the stars, making a larger inky patch in an already-black sky.

He had to guard against vertigo when he had no easy landmarks to fly by. Pilots could die after mistaking which direction was up while flying at night, and here he was planning to dodge and maneuver to get away from whatever was flying with them in the night sky. His stomach turned, lying to him about which way was up, as he righted the aircraft to fly level and straight by searching out and aligning to the dim horizon.

The red flecks of light appeared dead ahead and leveled out, dropping from above to match their altitude. "Fire, Moreau!"

The machine gun lit up as Jackson pulled up to align the gun with the glimmer he'd seen. Bless the Brits who'd invented tracer bullets and delivered the invention to the Aerodrome mere weeks before. War tended to produce new tools, and tracers made it much easier to aim both day and night. Jackson saw the trail of light stream out from the gun, providing dim illumination of their path as gunfire ripped through the night sky. Rounds hit and sparked off their target. The dim light of the tracer rounds lit up a winged shape as it approached them head-on.

Jackson eased the stick to the left as Moreau sent regular bursts from the gun toward the shape closing with them at high speed. Finally, the shots hit something solid again and set off another shower of sparks as both the regular rounds and the tracers pounded their target. Whatever they'd hit disappeared into the darkness.

Rather than risk a hard bank and the loss of airspeed that went with it, Jackson eased into a wider turn to scan above and below for the target. He knew of no engines quiet enough to do what he'd seen, unless the reckless pilot had shut his engines off completely for a dive at him. None of it made sense.

As before, the attack surprised him, coming from an impossible direction for the target Moreau had shot. The only possibility was that he had more than one opponent stalking him in the darkness, and these opponents could follow him better than he could follow them. The tail of his aircraft lurched to the side from the impact, and the controls at his feet and in his hands jerked momentarily.

Rudder control felt too loose and lost its responsiveness. To correct for a pull to the right, he eased the stick to the left to keep a straight and level flight path. Whoever his opponent was, he knew the night far better than Jackson. With unknown damage to the plane, it was time to scrub the mission. Now, his only goal was to escape whatever enemy flew with him in the sky. Without a good visual sighting and a description of what he had come across, the best he could report was unknown winged attackers showing flickers of red in the darkness. So far, he suspected at least two attackers to account for the approach angles, but he had no idea if that was all. The initial contact, a quick glimpse of red light, could have been a third opponent. That many skilled night fliers formed a dire situation in need of immediate attention, but he first had to survive the trip home.

He needed more speed, and he was already at full throttle. He dropped to less than fifty feet above the treetops, hoping against hope he'd gotten the rise and fall of the dark landscape right. Otherwise, he could fly straight into a hillside or a tree as he wove a deceptive path home. This low, the enemy couldn't see him silhouetted against the starry night sky. That must be how they'd found him, but then again, they'd attacked from above. The facts were a jumbled mess of contradictions, impossible to put together into an understandable image in his head. Some critical bit of information was missing, preventing him from piecing it all together to find a clear and rational explanation for the situation.

Whatever he'd run into, he outdistanced it as he retreated as fast as the damaged airplane could fly. It pained him to scrub the search for the downed aircraft by retreating, but he felt a small satisfaction at having run into whatever enemy force had brought down the missing airplane and surviving. The mission hadn't been a total failure. He and Moreau now carried critical information.

The pre-dawn glow of morning appeared and grew as he struggled to keep a straight course. Finally, the sun rose as they crossed back into France. A glance to the rear showed the rudder in tatters. He fought the broken rudder all the way home, burning through most of his reserve fuel in his rush to get back to the Aerodrome at Le Bourget.

As far as landings went, he and Moreau survived, despite the impressive wheel dents he put into the field. Any landing you walked away from was good enough to call a success.

Jackson rested his forehead against the padded edge of the cockpit. "Am I crazy, or did you see what I saw? No engines. Only wings, and that red glow, almost like a pair of eyes."

"I have seen nothing like it before. It sounds like something from my grandmother's stories, told to scare us into staying in bed at night. Be good, or the monsters will eat you. Still, more than one man has called you crazy before, if that helps." The Frenchman gave a subtle nod to the approaching ground crews and chuckled.

"How am I going to put this into a report that makes any kind of sense? The best I can do is say it was dark and I don't know what hit us, and that makes me sound clueless and blind. Anything more detailed, and they'll ground us for being too stupid to fly."

Jackson pulled a cigar from his breast pocket and chewed on it as he surveyed the damage to the tail of the Avro 504. Whatever they'd run into, it wasn't another airplane. Three clear slash marks cut their way through the canvas of the fuselage in a single swipe. He'd seen similar marks from machine gun fire, but no shots had been fired back at them. He'd heard no engine noise, either. Something striking the body of his airplane had been the first indication of trouble. That was hit number one. He held out three fingers and ran them along the damage to the frame and canvas.

Moreau stood at the tail, holding up the dangling controls for the rudder, half of which no longer hooked to anything. The controls ended in a serrated cut unlike anything he'd ever seen produced by bullet impacts or explosives. As he lifted a loose piece to examine it up close, the entire rudder fell off into his hands. Hit number two had nearly ruined the rudder. They were lucky to have made it back at all. Any hard maneuvers, and they could have spiraled into the ground as another lost airplane and crew.

Men ran up from several directions, pointing and shouting to each other.

Jackson let out a breath of relief at their narrow escape. "Good thing the airplane held together all the way back. I've done a little trick flying before, but the more parts you lose, the harder it gets to stay in the air." As their track had run along the same path taken by the missing plane and crew, he could narrow the location of the attack to within two or three miles on a map. There was no doubt in his mind now that the things he'd fought were the cause of the missing plane's disappearance. The attackers had to have taken the airplane down with their unexpected appearance. He had no real description of his attackers, but now he had a location, and he could make it back to the same place easily. "They flew a Farman MF.11, didn't they?"

"Oui," answered Moreau. "The ugly brown one with the cat painted on the side."

Where Jackson's Avro 504 had sleek lines, the Farman was a box with two seats and a wooden latticework for a tail. The engine was mid-plane, unlike his preferred front-mount engine. Those differences might matter when figuring out how he and Moreau had survived, while the other plane didn't. "What would happen if the Farman got hit on the back end, like we did when we nearly lost the rudder? They had no canvas covering." He had an idea but wanted Moreau's opinion to see if it matched.

"Not good. Break any of the main braces, and the whole tail might come off."

"We were lucky. Our first hit only tore out some minor supports, but the canvas held it all together. We have a little more structure in the tail as well, hidden under the skin." The Farman had nothing but main structural pieces, each critical to holding the tail on, and all exposed to view from any direction.

"Moreau, do me a favor. Get all the gawkers out of here. If they're not here to fix the plane, I don't want them around." There was no sense starting rumors or encouraging wild speculation. Maybe it only looked like an animal attack, and it was really something else, something more ordinary he hadn't figured out yet. He was a long way from convincing himself, but he couldn't file a report claiming a large, mysterious flying creature had tried to eat his rudder and nearly brought down his plane. Instead, he carefully cataloged his facts on the damage and what few visual details he remembered from glimpses in the dark. Even speculation over whether aircraft could perform well enough with engines off was too much conjecture. Straight facts and observations would stand or fall on their own.

French speech flew back and forth for a few moments, but soon only one man remained with Jackson and Moreau. He had a notepad and pencil, and he circled the biplane, shaking his head while making notes with his grease-blackened fingers. As the head mechanic, he knew each of the planes inside and out. If anyone could get this machine back in the air quickly, it was him. The man was a wizard with the wire, wood, and canvas making up most of the airplane body.

The mechanic slid his pencil into his pocket and shook his head. *"Quel travail!"* The way he said it made his meaning clear. It wouldn't be an easy fix. Easy or not, Jackson needed the plane.

"Moreau, please let him know we need it fixed as soon as possible. We can't afford to be on the ground, and we can't take a plane from another crew without canceling missions. I don't care how ugly it is, so long as it flies."

"Very well, Jackson. I will speak with him."

"You do that. I have a report to file." The reports seemed endless to Jackson. "I'll find a way to write it up, so I don't look stupid or crazy in front of Colonel Dubois, or the others who see the report when it goes up the chain." This one would undoubtedly be telegraphed back to the area coordinating offices. Nearly losing a second American observer inside a week would get the attention of people Jackson would rather not have to deal with.

Jackson stiffened to attention in Colonel Dubois' office, and the Frenchman fired off rapid questions as he leaned against his desk with his arms folded. "What was it?"

"I don't know, sir. It attacked from behind both times it hit us."

"A new *avion*?"

"It is possible the enemy has a new airplane model, but I don't know, sir. It was a moonless night. I heard no engines besides our own. I only got a glimpse of red lights." Lights that seemed to be glowing eyes, but Jackson knew better than to bring that up.

Colonel Dubois made a scoffing sound. "You are not quite an ace, no? A good pilot. Yet it surprised you."

"Yes, sir. Despite listening for engines both before and after the first encounter, I heard nothing. In theory, gliders or airplanes with their engine turned off could pose such a threat, but that's all speculation on my part, since I couldn't make a positive identification." With no ability to identify it by sight or by hearing, what did the colonel expect? That he would recognize his enemy by smell?

"There is much you do not know here. What do you know?"

"I know whatever it is, it would be devastating for the Central Powers to have a new weapon that can take down airplanes on a moonless night with little or no warning. This is a bigger discovery than their troop movements. It could revolutionize how we fight in the air, just as we're warming up to the idea of aerial combat."

John M. Olsen

"Bah. Air combat. Men fight to conquer ground, not to conquer air. Air blows where it will, and none control it. It will always be so."

There was no way in the world he would tell the skeptical colonel how important aircraft could become if they continued to get bigger and faster, as they had recently. Now was not the time. He also held his peace on what he really thought about the attack. It hadn't been an airplane or glider, but he still didn't know what it was. Moreau had hit it with gunfire. Sparks had ricocheted off stone or metal. Whatever they were, they were durable. He knew of nothing that fit all the parameters he held inside his head.

"With your permission, sir, I'll send my report of the incident to my Allied contacts to see if they've heard similar reports from other bases sending aircraft over the border into Belgium." Maybe some analyst desk jockey could make something of it. Spending more time with the colonel was a complete waste.

"Very well, Lance Corporal Jackson. Report it through your American chain of command. Me, I must replace your failed scouting mission with another."

"If I might, sir, I would recommend routing around our encounter zone if you wanted to see whatever's on the far side of that unsettled area." Colonel Dubois liked to count his resources like chess pieces. It wouldn't hurt to remind him that his pawns would disappear at that spot on the game board.

"Yes, of course. Now I must work out a schedule, with two *avions* missing from my resources. My superiors did not warn me they were so fragile. You are dismissed."

Jackson ground his teeth as he left the office. Fragile? The airplane had taken two direct hits and still made it home. With the interview over, it was time to stow his annoyance with Colonel Dubois and file his formal report. A report with clinically precise details, and no supposition, no implication, and absolutely no mention of flying creatures with glowing red eyes. Just a raw description of the events.

With luck, he and Moreau wouldn't be grounded long with the repairs. There were men missing out there, and they deserved his best efforts.

Call-up

My Dearest Pearl,

Our last mission was a success, although it was quite ordinary, compared to the forces fighting on the front lines and in the trenches. My squad helped some local soldiers and took care of a minor issue they'd run up against in their training. I can't really go into a lot of detail, for security reasons. I may have a few days to catch the nearby sights in France before my next assignment.

I wish you were here to see the French countryside with me, but it's not safe enough for you to visit yet. When the war is over, maybe we can save up enough money to take a trip. I'm sure you would love to see the old museums and cathedrals. There are sculptures on the streets, and I hear that in Paris, there are painters lining the Seine River capturing the scenery. If I can, I'll bring a painting home for you. I'm so close to Paris here that it would be a shame to miss out on a chance to bring something home to share with you.

If only I could hold you in my arms and tell you about the sights here and my hopes for the future.

John M. Olsen

I want to share everything I've seen here, but even more, I think always of your touch, your voice, and your gentle eyes. You inspire me to do my best, no matter what my assignment is. There is so much to tell you, and I can't possibly fit it all in a simple letter. My words can't do justice to how much I love you.

I hope you're feeling better. The last letter I got from you was a month ago, and you mentioned feeling under the weather. When you feel down, remember our last dance together, surrounded by friends and listening to that new brass band that had come into town. Ignore the part where I tried to sing along with the band. Maybe someday I'll be able to carry a tune.

Always remember you're my sun, my moon, and my everything. My love knows no bounds, and when I see you, I will sweep you off your feet and carry you away.

Don't worry for me. The fighting is far from where I sit tonight, and I'm doing well.

I know you think the way I sign my letters is funny, but I'm too used to the formalities of the military. One of these days, I'll write you a properly romantic letter, and sign it just George, and you won't know it's from me.

*I long to tell you more of what I've been up to,
but this will have to do for now.*

With love, forever and always,

Sgt. George Jones, USMC

S ergeant Jones sat at a small table as he finished writing his latest letter to his wife, who sat safe and sound back home in the outskirts of Chicago. Ashes drifted in the room's tiny hearth, remnants of letters he would never send now that he'd composed his latest missive to replace them.

He sealed the envelope and gently kissed it, then set it aside to go out in the morning mail.

A firm hand rapped on his door as he wrote out his home address below Pearl's name. The hotel room was temporary, as were most things in the Great War, but this hotel housed several Allied officers, as well as providing rooms for others, as needed, for the Americans' unofficial support of the war effort. Few knew exactly how many combat-ready men America had in Europe to observe the war as it degraded, but even fewer knew of him and his team.

His dreams of a week of downtime evaporated with the knock, as it usually did. The knock repeated. Despite being in a quiet town halfway between the front lines and Paris, he should have known it wouldn't last. He opened the door to see a fresh-faced private, who saluted with far too much enthusiasm. Jones returned the salute and eyed him up and down. "Yes, what is it, Private?"

"Telephone call for you, sir. We installed one just off the lobby. It's from our coordinating office across town."

It was nice to see they'd spared no expense when it came to communication. The Allied Forces might even win this war if they could ever figure out what to do about that horrible no-man's-land at the front, made up of Central and Allied trenches filled with some of the worst human conditions imaginable. But that was a job for the ordinary troops. If he had a telephone call, it was guaranteed not to be ordinary. "Show me where to take the call."

The private rushed off, forcing Jones to match the quick pace. If he'd learned anything, it was that rushing rarely solved problems. If you planned a job properly up front, there was no need to flail around in a rush to get things done. The better approach was to slip in, silent as the night, destroy the target, and slip back out before anyone noticed. In practice, it rarely worked out so nicely.

In a small dining area off the main lobby, the private showed him to a table with a boxy black telephone leaning against the wall. He picked up the earpiece and sat so he could speak into the fixed microphone. "This is Sergeant Jones."

A tinny voice on the other end said, "Sorry to interrupt your break, but we got a telegram. We're activating Special Unit 13, your rifle squad particularly. Come in and we'll fill you in."

"Can you give me anything now? It might take a day to round up the boys."

"Telephone lines are great, but they're not secure. You understand the security risk, do you not?"

"Right. I'll be there. Do you mean tonight, or in the morning?"

"What do you think, Sergeant? I've flagged this one as a high priority. It could be something normal and easily explained, but I doubt it. We need to identify it to make sure. I'll see you in three hours. I've already got people out rounding up the rest of your team." So much for giving the boys a few more hours of respite. They deserved rest and recovery time more than he did, especially with the loss of two members of the team so fresh in their memories.

The stress and trauma of their previous mission weighed heavily on the whole team, and the men deserved a break. They needed time to grieve. It wouldn't have been as bad if the two men had left bodies behind, but they were gone without so much as an identification tag left to note their passing. He had nothing to send home to their grieving families.

No sense dwelling on the past. Their line of work required action more than introspection. Some things couldn't wait a month, or even a day. After every mission, it seemed, he barely had time to sit down before the next emergency raised its head and demanded his attention. The lack of time to sit and plan annoyed him every time. The cost was often high, in both resources and lives, but it was worth it to keep the world free from menaces most people only dreamed of in their worst nightmares.

It was time to jump into the fire once again to save humanity from dangers they should never have to know about. At least the lucky ones would never learn of the horrors lurking in the dark. The lucky ones like Pearl, his wife, could continue to believe the world was a kind and caring place. Sergeant Jones wasn't lucky enough to live a blissfully ignorant life, and neither were his men.

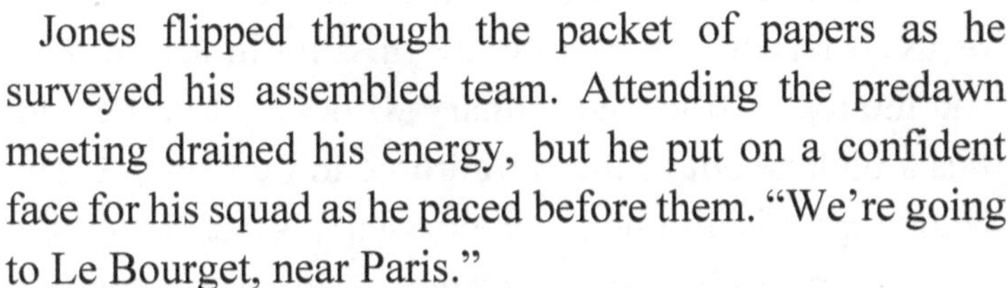

Jones flipped through the packet of papers as he surveyed his assembled team. Attending the predawn meeting drained his energy, but he put on a confident face for his squad as he paced before them. "We're going to Le Bourget, near Paris."

One of the men faked a French accent. "Ah, Paris! Oui, oui!"

"Knock it off, Davis. Nobody's going to Paris. We're stopping in Le Bourget because of a problem deep inside Belgium. A report came in, and one of our men flagged it as unusual. Maybe it's not supernatural, but it's too far outside normal parameters for us to ignore, so we're being sent to investigate."

Corporal John Miller, the grenadier and leader of Fireteam 1, yawned, then spoke. "Sir, if the problem is in Belgium, why are we going to Le Bourget?" The man was soft-spoken, but was an excellent fireteam leader. Behind his back, some of the men called him Brother Miller because of his religious upbringing.

"I'm still going through the details, but Le Bourget is where our witnesses are."

Davis piped up again. "Great. More witnesses to deal with. What do we use to pay off le witnesses this time to keep them quiet?"

"Maybe I should rephrase that. There are two survivors for us to talk to. Two more are missing in action. I've read the report from the primary witness, a Marine who flies a biplane out of the Aerodrome in Le Bourget. The whole report is all precision, crossed T's and dotted I's, with the most clinical description of an encounter I've ever read. Every bit of information he can pack into a report, and no speculation. I have to meet this guy. He's either clueless, or he's terrified of someone thinking he's a crank. Either way, he's given a lot of detail, if you know how to read between the lines."

Davis, an endless font of questions, asked, "What's your guess, sir? What is it we're hunting this time?"

"That's the problem. Given the description, we don't have enough information to classify whatever it is. The encounter was while flying at night, and they got surprised. We know that the attacker also flies, possibly has glowing red eyes, can maybe survive direct gunfire, and has claws with a span about a foot across. Lastly, it likes to chew on airplane rudders. I had to piece that together from a highly noncommittal report that reads like the author didn't want to get locked up in the nuthouse."

"Glowing red eyes as in reflecting light back at you, or as in summoned demon glowing red eyes?" Davis dropped his French accent to ask the question, a sure sign of worry.

"Like I said, the report is from a flight in the middle of the night. Not much light to be reflected. Take that how you want, but make sure you're ready for a fight."

The room sat in silence as everyone absorbed the sparse details.

"Here are your assignments. Fireteam 1, standard load-out, but pick up anything extra you think might help based on the description I've given. Fireteam 2, I'm assigning you to haul a radio along with us. We'll drop a second radio at the Aerodrome in Le Bourget. I want to keep in contact with the Aerodrome to coordinate with them. They tell me this portable radio station will do the trick. The mountains interfere, so I don't think we'll have a strong enough signal to reach all the way back here, but the Aerodrome can relay telegrams for us. Fireteam 3, Anderson and Davis." Jones glared at Davis as if daring him to speak up. Fireteam 3 accounted for both their recent losses, through no fault of their own, and they were still down two men, half their original group. "Standard load-out. You'll focus on recon and perimeter."

Corporal White spoke up for Fireteam 2. "Moore and Thomas, you'll haul the radio. That puts us a little light on sappers, sir. Can Fireteam 1 make up for that with some adjustments?"

Jones glanced over to Corporal Miller to speak for his team. "Can you cover that, Miller?"

"Yes, sir. Wilson will stock up on explosives to compensate."

Wilson laughed. "Oh, I'll stock up, all right. After the last two missions, I don't go anywhere without as much TNT as I can carry. May Alfred Nobel ever be blessed for his invention."

Working to keep the short fireteam involved, Jones turned to Corporal Anderson. "Make sure we have transportation. Get us a vehicle. Get two if you can't find something big enough for all of us and our gear. I think I saw armored vehicles of some sort over in the motor pool. Just make sure there's room for everything. Strapping our gear on top will work if it has to. We can make a caravan of it."

"Yes, sir."

"You each have your assignments. Meet back at the motor pool with everything packed and ready to go by noon. Count on having to carry all your gear for the last leg of the trip. I'll make sure the radio is waiting for us. Dismissed."

Despite the emotional wear and tear, and the physical exhaustion of non-stop missions, his squad knew their jobs and mustered their enthusiasm as they filed out into the predawn to prepare for the trip.

At a borrowed desk in the command offices, Jones reviewed the pilot's report one more time. Miller sat with him to act as a sounding board, and he used fingers to tick off his points as he reviewed the information for Jones. "The people at the Aerodrome clearly lacked details. We've got no physical description of the attacker, beyond having wings and claws. We have a description of the damage to the airplane. Is that it? Are you sure this is a job for a rifle squad from Special Unit 13?"

Jones shrugged. "There's a chance it could be something normal, and if that's the case, we get off easy this time. It would be a first. If it sounded suspicious enough to send our way, we treat it as a major threat, so we don't underestimate the enemy. If that's all we have, how can we get more information? They have more airplanes, don't they?"

"Yes, sir. They may be able to get eyes out there during the day to see if there's anything suspicious. At least during the day, they'll be able to see anything that comes after them. It's a win-win, so long as they make it back."

Jones nodded and made a note. "Good. I'll get a request sent in for them to do a daytime reconnaissance run." Jones hated to pull strings and owe favors, but he'd earned enough of a reputation with his command chain that they'd give him what he wanted if it wasn't too outrageous.

Miller tapped a finger on the report as he thought for a moment, then said, "I heard some of those airplanes have cameras. Maybe they can get a few photographs for us, too. I hate to rely on what someone remembered buzzing along several hundred feet off the ground, even if he's a trained observer."

"Good idea. This place is isolated by the terrain. The maps might not show us anything useful, but pictures will. They have the speed to get in and out fast. If it's as isolated as they say, there won't be any enemy aircraft to worry about. They'll be done and enjoying an evening in town before another team could get anywhere close on the ground." Timely information could make all the difference when putting boots on the ground in the area. Jones hated jumping into anything blind.

"Why the radio, sir? Was that something that came with our orders, or did you add that one?"

"I made the requisition. There are two reasons. One is the speed of relaying information back home through Le Bourget. Second, I figured if something's taken a liking to attacking airplanes on two out of two missions to the area, we may be able to coordinate with the aviators, and draw out whatever it is."

"Use them as bait?" Miller asked.

"Yes. But I'll make sure our pilot friend knows that's the part he's playing. He isn't just something to dangle out there to get what we want. I've read reports on maneuvers with combined air and ground forces helping each other. With the radio, we can call in and get them overhead within two hours, where it might take two days to hike out and back with reinforcements. The radio changes the whole dynamic on gathering information and transmitting orders. It won't help us gather information any faster, but it can get information from one place to another instantly, and I like that."

If he worked things right with the radio, he could save days. Maybe he could save lives, too. There was no evidence or proof either way on the state of the two men who'd gone down in the area. He factored in the idea that there might be a rescue mission added to his task to identify and destroy anything suspicious.

Jones composed a message to go back to the Aerodrome, addressed to Colonel Charles Dubois, the man in charge of the site. His message insisted on a daytime mission with a camera to take high altitude pictures. He set the message aside, having one more task to handle first.

It wouldn't be his first time pulling rank through an appeal up the chain, but he had to get approval from the head of Special Unit thirteen to impress and motivate the French colonel. He dashed off the approval request, then waited. Soon, everything was scheduled, underway, and proceeding in good order.

Something was bound to go wrong. It always did, and generally at the worst possible moment.

Sergeant Jones pulled his three fireteam leaders aside to an office for a quick conference at the motor pool as the supplies were loaded onto a pair of armored cars.

"I sent off a telegram to Colonel Dubois before coming over here, asking him to have aerial photographs ready by the time we arrive this evening. He was reluctant to schedule the flight, but he finally agreed to help after I leaned on him a little. It's not much, but it'll at least tell us about the terrain. With a little luck, they'll spot something useful. If all else fails, it'll give us an idea of the best paths to use hiking in."

Corporal Miller, the leader of Fireteam 1, raised a finger. "If they've got these airplanes, can't they take us all the way to the target?"

Jones shook his head. "There's nothing big enough to hold all of us and our gear, and there's probably no clear space to land. It's rough old-growth forest. We can probably drive most of the way, so long as we don't run into issues at the border." Issues like enemy forces and firefights. Allies could be a problem, too, but they wouldn't shoot at his squad.

Corporal White pointed a thumb at the cars being loaded. "At least they're expecting us. I hate showing up unannounced and having to come up with an excuse for being there."

Jones leaned against the utilitarian desk. "They should have food and lodging ready for us, but I suspect it'll be a big tent with cots."

John M. Olsen

White laughed. "I've had worse. A couple of meals and a cot to crash on will be fine by me, sir."

Some officers were more receptive than others when it came to visits and requests from Special Unit 13. A select few knew their charter and would do everything in their power to keep the special unit supplied and working. Others occasionally got in the way or made bad assumptions. The worst were those who had no idea what they were up against and threw up roadblocks at every opportunity out of a misguided sense of who should own what tasks. The latter group were always the ones to get in the way the most, or to suffer the worst casualties when things fell apart as they nosed around in things no sane human should have to deal with.

The pilot, Lance Corporal James Jackson, had written the initial incident report himself rather than relying on whatever summary report the colonel would have sent. That spoke both good of the pilot, and bad of the colonel. Jones decided to watch both men more closely until he had a better feel for them. The squad was down two team members, and he needed all the help he could get if this incident blew up on him.

Jones eyed Corporal Anderson, the leader of the half-team, the one that had lost two men. "I'll keep an eye on the Americans at the Aerodrome. If they can get pictures for us, we may be able to set up a good working relationship. Maybe even do a little recruiting. Everyone, make sure we're loaded and ready to go. I have one more phone call to make, then we leave."

His fireteam leaders left the small office as Jones eyed the telephone hanging on the wall. With the mostly-functional telephone network, there was one last thing Jones could do. He lifted the earpiece, turned a crank a few times, and asked to be connected to a friend working a desk job nearby in the complex. His friend Robert would be in his office now that the sun was up, and if anyone knew gossip, he would. His position put him in a crossroads of information, both official and under the table.

"Robert! I have a quick question for you."

"You know work discussions can't go over a line like this." It was a gentle reminder that the lines were too easy to monitor, even within the small base, and that only normal work should be discussed.

"No problem. I wanted to ask you about someone. What do you know about a Colonel Charles Dubois? He's running the Le Bourget Aerodrome."

Papers rustled on the far end of the line. "Ah, here we go. He's an old-time cavalry commander and a member of the French Foreign Legion."

"Like mechanized cavalry? New armored vehicles with machine gun mounts?"

"Sorry, more like horses and sabers." The tinny voice had an apologetic sound to it across the line.

"Great. We're working with airplanes and radios, and the colonel knows horses. Just what we need. Any idea how this guy got into this position at the Aerodrome?"

"Sorry, I'm just the messenger. I don't have a direct line to gossip about French officers."

First the sketchy information, and now a fossil of a commander to deal with. This mission was looking worse all the time.

Reconnaissance

The change in reconnaissance orders surprised Lance Corporal Jackson, mostly because of their rapid turnaround. In the military, paperwork took time, and change was slow. He hadn't expected anyone to so much as look at his report for another day or two, and now someone had responded, not only with orders that overrode Colonel Dubois, but with a team of Marines who were due to arrive at the Aerodrome by the end of the day. That wasn't what he'd expected, but he wouldn't complain at the help offered by a ground team.

The unfortunate part was that the orders had gone directly to Colonel Dubois, who'd immediately summoned Jackson and Moreau, lacking anyone else to blame for the new orders.

The colonel scowled as he sat at his desk. "You will requisition a camera and fly to the area of the attacks to take photographs. Moreau, you and Jackson know the location best. If you come back alive, the Americans will have the photographs they demand."

The conversation would go downhill in a hurry if Jackson didn't watch himself, so he chose his words with care. "We'll see to the details immediately, sir. Moreau can handle the camera, while I prepare the airplane." He might as well pretend it was the colonel's idea rather than rub salt into his wounded ego. "Do you have any further instructions before we prepare for the mission?"

"Only if you wish to set up a new tent for our visitors. I have no room for them, and they will arrive with their own equipment. Perhaps they will arrive and see there is nothing to be done, and leave."

Nothing started the day off right like a burr under the saddle of an old cavalryman. Not sure if he could trust that others would set things up properly, or even on time, Jackson offered a small olive branch. "As long as we're requisitioning the camera, I'll pick up a tent as well. You said they were sending a squad?"

"Oui, but not a full squad. Ten men and much equipment. They arrive later today in armored cars, after your mission to take photographs of the area. You are dismissed."

Jackson hurried out of the office. Outside, he led the way to the supply office, happy to pick up equipment for the team scheduled to arrive soon. With luck, this incoming team would be easier to work with than Colonel Dubois. "I'll handle the tent while you're getting everything you need for the camera. We can haul it over together, since I want to set up their tent near the airstrip."

Soon, Jackson was pulling a cart with both the tent and the aerial camera gear, and Moreau pushed from behind where he could safeguard the expensive camera equipment. Near the aircraft maintenance building, he flagged down some idle members of the maintenance crew, and handed off the tent, along with pantomimed instructions to set it up beside the building. The men gave him baffled looks.

"Moreau, can you make sure these gentlemen got my instructions right on where to set up this tent? It needs to be near our building, here, with the door facing out onto the field."

After a few exchanged words, Moreau smiled. "They tease, as you say. They already understand what to do. A little joke at the expense of the American."

"As long as it gets done, they can laugh at me all they want. I just don't want our guests to arrive without a place to stay." Jackson gave the men a good-natured wave and a smile. If this war lasted much longer, he would have to put real effort into learning to speak French. Few of the Frenchmen he worked with had any desire to learn English, so he understood and valued the privilege of having the bilingual Marcel Moreau as a flying partner.

John M. Olsen

With the bundled tent removed from the cart, all that remained was the camera. "How does the camera look, Moreau?"

"Ah. The K-1, it is good. I have used it before." He hefted the camera's film magazine, it was a good six inches wide.

Jackson and Moreau left the cart with the tent and carried the boxed camera to their temporary replacement plane which sat ready to go with its fuel topped off. Jackson's Avro 504 wouldn't be ready for another day or two yet, with its rudder repairs, although the torn side already bore a new patch sealed with canvas glue.

The loaner was a Farman MF.11, nearly identical to the missing airplane. It was an ungainly thing, but great for scouting. It bothered Jackson that such a fast plane hadn't been able to escape whatever had attacked the airplanes. This time he had the advantage of foreknowledge, and daylight to see by. He also didn't plan to fly below picture-taking altitude of five thousand feet unless he spotted something important. This was a mission to take pictures, not a combat sortie.

Then Jackson noticed something under the wings of the airplane. "Hey, Moreau. It's got bombs already mounted." Eighteen bombs sat in external mounts. The rear observer cockpit also held a swiveling machine gun, much different from the fixed forward gun mounted on top of his Avro 504.

"Bah. I prefer to make my own and drop them by hand, but I will make this one work if I must. But this trip is for photographs." Moreau patted the camera, now neatly attached to the outside of the observer cockpit and pointed down for a clear view of the terrain they would traverse.

The daylight flight held a slightly higher risk of being seen and chased by the enemy, as Jackson had explained to the colonel, but with light winds, a sunny sky, and the isolated nature of the planned path, he had only a few nagging worries left.

Central Powers forces were rumored to be nearby, based on the original reports of the missing team, but he'd seen nothing on earlier trips. Then there was the attacker that had downed one aircraft and damaged a second. The squad of Marines had to be interested in the attacks more than the information on enemy placements, since that was the only new piece of information available when the sudden interest appeared from headquarters. If someone was that interested, the situation might be more dangerous than he'd thought. Odds were good they knew something, or at least suspected something. Nobody sent a squad on next-day orders to check out something ordinary.

John M. Olsen

Once Jackson's inspection was complete, they took to the sky and climbed as he flew north. He leveled the aircraft off at cruising altitude for the trip into Belgium as he picked out his course using his compass and the landmarks far below. The exhilaration of flying made up for the earlier ire of Colonel Dubois.

His waypoint towns looked different during the day but guided his path just as well. At their higher altitude, Jackson couldn't see any details in the towns or forest, but that was what the camera was for. Rather than save the whole roll of film for the search zone, Moreau directed their flight path so he could use part of the film roll to take shots of each of the Belgian towns as they passed overhead. With a bit of luck, they might spot German or Prussian troops within the towns.

After more than an hour in the air, they crossed into the no-man's-land with no habitations—the area where the two attacks had taken place. Soon, he found the right area, and Jackson waved to Moreau to resume taking pictures. There was no way to guarantee they were on the exact same path, but they had to be close.

On a low rise among the ancient forested hills sat an old castle, an excellent landmark for verifying they were in the right spot, should they return later. No roads ran to it, or even anywhere nearby. It sat in isolation, unlike so many other old buildings he'd flown over on the way.

Moreau gave a signal to drop some altitude, so the pilot leveled off at two thousand feet for closer photos of the castle. Trees grew right against its walls, and the roof had seen better days. Green moss grew in large patches on the roof, and dark spots looked like holes where the roof had fallen in. It had to be abandoned.

Despite the lack of roads, it could be used as an enemy base, so the more detail they could gather, the better.

On Jackson's third pass over the ancient structure, Moreau slapped Jackson on the back and pointed. A quick search revealed trees snapped in half, and the crumpled fuselage of an airplane that had landed hard. With the obviously rough impact, there was less chance of survivors, but someone could still be alive down there.

No signals came from the ground despite their lower altitude and clear wing markings as a French aircraft.

Nothing attacked, either, which surprised Jackson. If the flying attackers were aircraft, there had to be an airbase nearby to intercept their intrusion. Had it really been something else, or had he let his imagination get the better of him, convincing him of an attack by a creature that couldn't exist? No, it was *not* an airplane. Of that he was certain.

Nothing man-made, other than the old castle, was visible for miles. No attackers, no gunfire from the ground. Nothing. What was the difference between the attacked flights and this trip to take pictures? As far as Jackson could tell, the only change was the sunshine. If it was a creature, what could it be? No giant nocturnal creatures came to mind, so all he could do was keep the plane stable for Moreau's photographs as he considered what might have come after them.

Once Moreau had the initial pictures he needed, Jackson dropped to just a thousand feet to look for more signs or signals. He saw nothing but a scattering of crumpled airplane pieces. The wings had been torn off as it hit the trees, and the forest floor showed a groove torn across the ground and underbrush by the impact.

They had the pictures they'd come for, so Jackson checked his time and fuel. They could still head deeper into Belgium and finish the original mission, to search out enemy troop movements. It might appease Colonel Dubois to have the additional intelligence. Jackson climbed back up to altitude and headed north over the low mountains.

On the far side lay more forested hills, but off in the distance, the haze took on a different tint. Pointing to direct Moreau's eyes, Jackson confirmed the anomaly with his partner and flew on. Soon, they spotted rough, ill-used roads and the occasional farmhouse. Roads improved the farther they went, until the change in the haze resolved into smoke from a camp.

Jackson didn't dare fly close, but the camera pointed straight down, unable to get a shot of the camp. That was easy enough to fix. He signaled Moreau to be ready with the camera shutter as he banked in a wide turn to aim the camera at the camp.

A quick glance back showed Moreau giving a thumbs-up, but glancing back toward the camp showed movement. An anti-aircraft gun showed a puff of smoke as it fired, and a few seconds later, an explosion blossomed in the sky nearby.

No photos would make it back to the Aerodrome if a flack cannon shot them out of the sky. Jackson completed his turn and headed for home.

Not only had they found the downed aircraft, they also had critical information on enemy troops, likely headed toward the front. If the troops took the most direct path, they might even pass near the old castle and the plane crash. Jackson added a new level of urgency to the return trip. If the enemy stumbled upon the castle and the airplane crash, they could capture any survivors. It was part of his job to deny advantages to the enemy, and there was a chance the visiting squad could get in to rescue any survivors before the enemy could arrive.

The longer a squad on the ground took, the less chance there was of any survivors making it out alive. He had to keep his hopes high and assume they were down there waiting for rescue despite all evidence to the contrary.

Then there were the mysterious creatures to consider. If they could be used as a war resource, he didn't want the enemy to get there first.

It was time to fly home with their precious payload of pictures. The film might not give him all the answers he wanted, but now they had the exact location of the wreck, and a sense of urgency on multiple fronts.

Photographs hung to dry in a temporary darkroom. The acrid, metallic smell of chemicals permeated the air. Jackson pulled a picture from its clip and gave it a close look in the dim red light as Moreau cleaned up the chemical baths. The picture showed the castle in wonderful detail, down to its crenellated walls, decorative sculptures, and damaged wooden roof. He moved down the line to find a good shot of the wreckage and pulled it from the drying line as well.

Jackson waved a hand toward the darkened electric lamp overhead. "Are we safe to turn this on now?"

"Oui. The images are developed. Good photographs. I told you the camera was exceptional."

"Good tools work better in good hands. I'll blame you for the good photographs, Moreau."

The pictures showed even more detail with the bright electric light turned on. Pictures taken from the lowest altitude were the best for looking over the wreckage and inspecting details of the castle, while the high-altitude images gave important information on the surrounding terrain.

The images of enemy troops hadn't fared nearly as well. The blur of a banked turn combined with the much greater distance of the shot rendered them useless for counting the size and composition of the enemy force. All Jackson knew was the precise location, and that the force was big enough to haul around anti-aircraft guns. The guns made them a significant threat.

Flipping back to the best photograph of the airplane wreckage, Jackson pulled out a magnifier. There was no mistaking the bare struts and structure of the crumpled

Farman MF.11 plane. "It's our missing plane, all right. I can even see the cat painted on the side."

He dropped the lens back into a drawer with a hopeful grunt. "I can't see any bodies." Even with the magnifier, the image lacked sufficient detail to tell if the two fliers lay dead nearby from the crash, so there was no proof of their deaths. That gave him hope.

Moreau shrugged. "Maybe they live, maybe not. I saw no signs or signals from the ground, but that changes nothing. We go again to find out. Where do we land?"

The high-altitude terrain picture told a grim story for any search for a landing spot. Dense trees ran through the whole area. There wasn't so much as a small lake to land a pontoon plane upon. "I've got nothing here. We can't land nearby."

"What of the castle?"

"That's no good. It's not a big castle, and there aren't any open fields around it. There aren't even any roads, and the inner courtyard is too small and overgrown. There isn't much underbrush, so it's fairly easy walking, but landing anywhere close to the castle would be the hard way, just like the Farman. We have to hand this mission off to infantry to hike in and do a ground search. I'm sure Colonel Dubois knows some French cavalry who could get there and look around if our visitors won't do it." Based on their relationship, Jackson didn't give the idea of help from the colonel any hope, despite his optimistic words. The colonel had already decided the men were gone and marked them off as a loss. There had to be a way to get people to the site. Even if the Farman flying team was dead, the men deserved to return home, at least to be buried rather than torn apart by wild animals.

Something caught his eye on the castle photo, now set aside on the table. "What are these lumps along the roof edge?"

"Ah, you have not visited many castles or cathedrals. We must fix this problem and show you the great old buildings. Even the waterspouts are impressive gargoyle sculptures. The buildings are art. I will show you when we fly over old buildings again, or you can visit Paris after the war."

The old castle had to be a key to the whole thing. It was the only structure within miles of the crash site, and it was also the approximate location of his own attack. "Look here, Moreau. The castle is only three stories tall, so it's not huge. I'd say it was more of a manor than a castle, if it wasn't for those crenellated roof edges. I don't see any signs of occupancy in or around the castle. No trails in or out are visible for a few miles, and there are no farms nearby. It's in a bad state of repair, but it's the only thing that adds up. I must be missing something here. How rare is it for a castle to be completely abandoned and forgotten? Maybe we need more pictures. Different angles to show how to get in and out."

"There are many abandoned castles. Many things here are old, unlike America, where your buildings are all new. Maybe we just find our people and leave it alone. It is old and empty. It falls apart. I do not like it." Moreau rubbed the back of his neck.

At least it wasn't just Jackson who'd gotten a case of the creeps from the old castle. "What sort of animals could live there and chew up our airplane? I've never seen a bird big enough to do something like that. I'm not ruling out the idea of giant birds, but it sends shivers down my back to think about it. Maybe some unknown creature, one the biologists haven't come across yet. Or maybe it's like the stories where crazy men built weird creatures to do their bidding, or someone breeding large attack birds."

"I hate the stories. Mr. Wells made a mockery of my family name with his book about a Dr. Moreau."

Jackson understood now why Moreau's name had sounded familiar, finally tying it to the book by H. G. Wells. His bombardier had dealt with people expecting him to be something other than what he was, all because of his name. He could sympathize with Moreau's position.

Everyone assumed Jackson was directly related to the great Andrew Jackson, and it just wasn't so. Expectations and reality rarely meshed well.

When it came to the flying creatures, Jackson was at a loss on what to expect, and he found himself unable to mentally map the situation to anything real. He was sure a simple explanation existed, but hadn't discovered one yet that fit the bizarre evidence before him.

Jackson sat across the table from Moreau, with their photos scattered across the scratched tabletop in the room that served as their office. He labored with his favorite fountain pen to fill out a report on their flight. Military life and paperwork always seemed to go hand-in-hand, but he'd run into a roadblock. "Moreau, do I write this for Colonel Dubois, or do I write it for the incoming team? They'll both get a copy. If it's for the colonel, I need to play up the chance for recovering the airplane, and the possibility of rescue comes second. If it's for the visiting squad, I'm not sure what they're after, or what I should focus on."

John M. Olsen

"Use simple facts and small words. It is best for footmen and cavalry both." Moreau grinned. The men flying over the ground forces looked down on their counterparts in more ways than one, but it was always with good humor.

That wasn't a bad idea. He had easy proof of the downed aircraft, and there was no clear evidence of bodies. The other photographs were available to fill in details on the local geography and the distance from the target to known enemy troops. Jackson scribbled away at the report now that he had a good sense of where it needed extra detail. There was no need to speculate on the attacks, since this mission report covered only the reconnaissance. As before, he would stick to nothing but the clear evidence of the photographs and his impartial observations. With luck, he would get a chance to make his case in person, to emphasize his desire and preference for a rescue mission. The airplane engine might be worth hauling out, but he doubted it.

Jackson's only real concern was rescue or recovery, and the longer they delayed, the more likely it would be a recovery mission to bring back two bodies. He had to keep his hopes up that they'd survived the crash. If both men were dead, he would become a laughingstock at the waste of time, effort, and resources, he was sure.

He finished his technical report with a flourish of a signature and set to writing out a duplicate. The military always wanted copies of everything, but in this case, he didn't mind. That meant the report would go to more than just Colonel Dubois.

"I'm glad you suggested straight facts and small words. I'm going to have to send this to follow my earlier report, and I don't know whose desk it'll end up landing on. Whoever it is, they were sharp enough to get someone on their way here, and to order the photos after my last message. With a little luck, they'll see where I'm headed with my information and make a sensible decision. I'm afraid they're going to butt heads with the colonel." So long as it didn't slow down search efforts, Jackson didn't mind the colonel getting his nose tweaked.

"But if they're on the way here, won't they miss the telegraph at the far end?"

Moreau had a point. Jackson pulled out another sheet of paper for a third copy to hand to the rifle squad due to arrive at any time. "More paperwork. You're enjoying this, aren't you?"

"But of course. You tie yourself into a knot when you have no control over what they choose."

Maybe Moreau was right, but he cared about the missing men, and would do whatever he could for them, even if the effort seemed futile. With the third copy complete, Jackson walked a copy over to the telegraph office and filled out more forms to send it on its way. The military wasn't known for speed or efficiency, but it was thorough. Now it was time to wait for the rifle squad to see if he could work with them any easier than with Colonel Dubois.

Approach

My Dearest Pearl,

I'm sorry my writing is so bad. I'm in a vehicle driving across France, and the road is bumpy. Rather than take time off like I had hoped, I've been unexpectedly given a new assignment. My squad will meet with some people to review recent reports for important information. You know me, always thrilled with government paperwork. Some people I will be working with are American, and some of them are French. I always feel the fool when I can't understand them. With my time here so far, the best I can do is pick out a few words. Bonjour. Oui. I've learned to ask where the bathroom is, but that's about it. Maybe they can send me and my team to language training so we can communicate better.

One of the men on my team is a linguist, so he helps out where he can. His parents emigrated from Europe and insisted he learn multiple languages growing up. Then there's Davis. He pretends to know French, and annoys everyone with how bad he is at it. I think he does it on purpose.

John M. Olsen

Of course, I'm still a master of the language of love, but only for you. Cupid has nothing on me. I hold a vision of you, lovely as ever, in my mind as I write to you. You are my harbor in the storm.

Hearing your voice and feeling your touch are my fondest memories, as well as my greatest of hopes.

With love forever and always,

Sgt. George Jones, USMC

Sergeant Jones eyed the buildings lining the grassy Aerodrome runway as Private Harris, one of his riflemen, drove the Peugeot armored car. As a linguist with a good grasp of the local language, Harris spoke to the Frenchmen at the roadblocks along the way, and at the entrance to the Aerodrome. He got them through the gates and to the Aerodrome's temporary offices without incident, but not without delays. It had taken most of the day to make the trip, and the sun edged low in the sky as evening approached.

"Don't bother unloading yet, boys. I don't know how long we'll be here. Hold tight while I check in."

The main office, such as it was, occupied a little more space than the other rickety temporary buildings. The buildings still smelled of fresh whitewash. The war itself felt more permanent than the buildings near the airstrip. Inside, he strode to a desk where a French enlisted man sat at a desk. This visit would take forever if he needed to grab Harris to translate everything for him.

Working up his best greeting, Jones came to attention before the desk and said, "Bonjour. Do you speak English?"

"A little bit. May I help you?"

Relief flooded Jones at the ability to communicate without a translator. The locals always said the same thing about speaking only a little, even if they spoke excellent English. Maybe they taught them to answer with 'a little bit' in school as the standard answer.

"I'm Sergeant George Jones, USMC. Colonel Dubois is expecting me and my rifle squad."

"A moment." The man stood and knocked on a door behind him, then poked his head through to rattle off something in French.

Returning to his desk, the man said, "The colonel will see you soon. Have a seat, sir."

Had the secretary emphasized the colonel's rank, or was it a trick of his accent? He hated power games, but it came as a package deal with much of the military, and especially when working with foreign forces.

Rather than sit, he held up a finger and poked his head out the door. "White! See if you can find the guy who wrote that report. Take Harris with you, but keep it casual and chummy. I may be a while." If the colonel wanted to play waiting games, Jones planned to keep the wheels rolling behind the scenes.

Satisfied, Jones took a seat and pulled out a knife to clean his fingernails. The secretary glanced over disdainfully, but said nothing, as Jones moved from one fingernail to the next with purposeful precision.

Minutes passed. Finally, Colonel Dubois opened his door and produced a fake smile that failed to reach his eyes. "Sergeant Jones. Welcome. Come in and tell me of your orders."

Things were about to get interesting, and the colonel wouldn't like the results. Wearing his own fake smile, he entered the office and stood before the colonel's desk when he wasn't offered a seat.

"What brings you to Le Bourget Aerodrome, Sergeant? Why have you come?"

"You saw the report that was sent to our advising group's office, sir? Our team has come to investigate, based on that report."

"We have no need of your investigation. A plane and two men were lost in a tragic accident. I have allowed your superiors to order aerial photographs. You may collect them."

"My plan is to investigate the situation. It will require more than collecting photos. I want to see whatever evidence there is to be seen and talk to everyone involved as part of my investigation."

"I'm afraid we are very busy. This Aerodrome is a critical resource for the war. I cannot do more than reserve a little space for you until you are prepared to leave, and I must insist you schedule all interviews through my office. I am surprised a rifle squad was given a job such as this. Your skills in combat seem a poor match for this investigation. I can assure you, the situation has been entirely resolved."

Jones worked to keep his building temper bottled up. "I'm not sure you understand the full significance of my visit, Colonel." Jones retrieved the letter he had hoped he wouldn't need. The one with General Ferdinand Foch's signature, alongside that of General of the Armies John "Black Jack" Pershing underneath French and English instructions. The level of cooperation and briefings necessary to create the letter had taken months, but both military leaders had agreed to the necessity when given top secret evidence of the purposes of Special Unit 13.

"You will find that this letter gives me clear authority to do as I have asked. I phrased it as a request out of courtesy. As stated in the letter, you will make any and all accommodations until my mission here concludes." Things always worked better when locals helped because it was the right thing to do, but Jones felt the need to rush this mission along, even if it ruffled a few feathers.

After reading through the letter, Colonel Dubois folded the paper and returned it to its envelope before handing it back. "I see. What *requests* do you have of me and my Aerodrome?" He sounded as though he'd just eaten a lemon, and his expression soured to match.

"I will interview your pilot and bombardier, then decide if we require any more time or resources. I understand you are a busy man, so thank you for taking the time to meet me, Colonel. Is there anything else you wish to know while I'm already here?" It always paid to be polite, even after rubbing the colonel's nose in the news that he had little say in the matter.

"No. I will, of course, consider your every request. You are dismissed."

Consider? The colonel had an ego even after Jones had deflated it with the end-run leverage of the military commander at the top of the colonel's chain of command. There would be no helpful dialog here, but Jones always got what he needed in the end. Jones could already imagine the complaint letters the home office was about to receive from the colonel. That always happened when he had to deal with people who didn't qualify for a full debriefing. Eventually he'd need to defend his actions, but his chain of command knew of his skills, and tolerated his impatient nature. It was part of the game, and Jones had played it for years.

Overall, the conversation with Colonel Dubois could have gone a lot worse. Jones made his way back out to the team waiting with the armored cars on the dirt road running end-to-end through the camp. Corporal White, Fireteam Two's leader, said, "We found our man, and we put a hold on his telegraph report until you've given it a look, sir. Here's the copy he made for you." White handed over the paper. "Once you've reviewed it, I'll take you to the office where we found the pilot and bombardier. They've even set up a tent for us next to their building."

The report was as clinical and dry as the first one, trying to dance around the oddities, and not always succeeding. The descriptions of the photographs intrigued him, and he looked forward to setting his eyes on the actual images.

At the bottom of the report, he added a few coded words and changed the destination to a different office before handing it back to White. "Please replace the other telegraph with this one and send it immediately." Based on the information he already knew, they would leave the Aerodrome and make their way into Belgium soon. It wouldn't do at all to leave the Special Unit 13 brass in the dark about where they'd gone and what he expected to find.

White sent one of his men running to the telegraph office, then waived Jones forward deeper into the camp. "I'll take you to meet the report writer now, sir."

He looked forward to the next stop on his walk-around, where he would finally get to meet the pilot. "Does he have the photographs with him?"

"Oh, yeah. Pretty good shots, but not good enough to identify what tore up the downed airplane. Are we going to the crash site?"

"Of course, but not until we've squeezed all the information we can out of our witnesses. It could turn out to have an ordinary explanation, but the more I see, the more it feels funny to me. I've learned to trust my gut on these things when it starts to smell of the unnatural."

"In here, sir." White held a door open into one of the nondescript whitewashed buildings.

Inside, Harris stood at attention with a grim expression, doing his best to intimidate the two men at the desk, but not really pulling it off. "Thank you, Private." Harris had joined Special Unit 13 just weeks before because of his unique combination of linguistics skills and having not only survived an attack by a minor summoned demon, but managing to kill it with nothing but an electric lamp's power cord and a broken chair. Creativity counted for something when you never knew what you might run into next. Besides knowing passable French, he was fluent in German and multiple Dutch dialects, primarily because of his immigrant parents.

Based on the uniforms of the two seated men, he identified his fellow Marine and the Frenchman, so he addressed the American. "It's time we cut through to the core of the matter. I need to know everything you didn't put into your reports." Jones pulled a chair away from the wall and sat across the desk from them.

The two men glanced at each other as if confirming whether they wanted to spill the beans or continue with the sanitized version. With clear reluctance, the American said, "I'm not sure what you mean."

At their hesitation, Jones continued. "Let me break the ice. I've seen things out there that would curl your hair. Things nobody should ever see. Your report leaves out anything you think might make you look crazy. Tell me the crazy parts."

"Will this go into any reports?"

"Not that can be tied to your records, and definitely not to Colonel Dubois." Jones' special permissions letter could work wonders in losing certain paperwork when it became necessary.

The relief on both their faces was palpable. They'd seen something, and they were scared to talk about it. He was on the right track.

"We never got a close look. The weirdest part was when we shot one."

"Shot one of them? There were several? How many?" That hadn't been clear from the report, but that ramped up the importance. If someone had created or summoned several things, their job had just become more difficult to straighten out.

"Right. Based on flight paths during the fight, one creature couldn't have both attacked our tail and been in front of us moments later. That means at least two, but possibly three. Our gun is a fixed front-facing mount. The regular and tracer rounds bounced and sparked off whatever they hit. It flashed past us too quickly to see details in the dark. Our only light was starlight."

"What do you *think* attacked you?"

Jackson shook his head. "I don't know. I haven't seen anything that fits."

"Not an airplane?"

"No. That's the one thing I can be sure of. It wasn't an airplane that hit us."

"Let me see your pictures."

Jackson spread a set of six-inch contact prints out on the table, along with a couple of enlarged photos. The Frenchman sat silently beside him, taking in the conversation.

Jones whistled and looked over to the Frenchman. "Nice work on the pictures, by the way."

The Frenchman warmed at the compliment and said, "Thank you, sir. The camera is a joy."

Joy or not, the photos showed the downed aircraft among the trees, and gave a good view of the lay of the land. "Any word on survivors?"

John M. Olsen

"No, sir. No bodies or survivors visible in the photograph, and no sign or attempt to contact us when we flew over for the pictures. Will you be staging a rescue attempt?"

"Yeah, we're going to pay the site a visit." He didn't tell them the rescue took second place to identifying and neutralizing whatever creature they'd run into. A visit in-person was the only way to get to the bottom of it, since the photos showed no signs of habitation, human or otherwise.

"What can we do to help? We typically run air support near the trenches and do surveys from the air. I can fill you in on our capabilities."

Sergeant Jones scratched his chin in thought. "I don't know exactly what I need yet, but we've got a Guglielmo Marconi radio to leave here at the Aerodrome, and one to take with us. If we need something, we can call it in."

The Frenchman's eyes grew wide. "A Marconi? Fantastique! If only one would fit into the airplane."

There were advantages to having a budget that allowed for the newest gadgets. All he had to do was make sure he had the men to use them and demonstrate the need. Other squads within Special Unit 13 had it even better with advanced prototype weapons, but the procurement office hadn't seen fit to send him the newest and best of everything on this mission.

Maybe there was a way to use these two men after all. He would keep them in mind. It might annoy Colonel Dubois, but Jones figured putting these two in charge of the Aerodrome side of the radio link might keep Special Unit 13's work more isolated. He wanted to avoid bringing in the Aerodrome's leadership. Specifically, the colonel would remain in the dark as long as possible. Preferably forever.

Jones stood. "Let's get the radio base station unloaded and tested. If you think there may be survivors, we'd better not wait until tomorrow morning."

As his men tested the radio connection, Jones observed from the top of the armored Peugeot, a canteen in hand, as a light evening breeze brought scents of the greenery surrounding the Aerodrome's fields. He turned to Corporal Miller. "Any fresh ideas on what we're facing based on the new evidence? With the latest report and the photos, I still can't make out whether it's something we've seen before, or a new cryptid."

John M. Olsen

Miller leaned against the driver's door of the armored car and looked up to acknowledge the question from Jones. "I don't know, Sarge. My paranoid nature says it's more than an obscure creature like Bigfoot popping up from hiding. It feels like someone went to the trouble to summon a creature, which means it's bad news. Real bad."

"You're probably right, except it's several creatures, from what we've learned. I've heard of lots of creatures in mythology that fly and have glowing eyes. Some of those creatures carry a real grudge against humanity. I got a list of possibilities from the eggheads, just in case." He had to be prepared to deal with any and all comers. "Everyone knows the more common things. Wyverns, dragons, dire mutations of birds, winged demons." Variations and possibilities danced through his thoughts as he itemized the strengths and weaknesses of each.

Miller laughed. "No wonder you pulled out so much equipment. We're going to have a hard time hauling all that stuff on our backs. I hate to expand your list of options, but don't forget creatures tied to cultists. The idiots keep thinking this time they'll get the summoning right, and everything will work out, even though it never has before. Sometimes I wonder if I'd have had a bigger impact sticking with my training to be a priest. Keep the idiots from summoning things in the first place by converting them."

"Bullets stacked up against preaching? I'll take bullets every time, if you want quick results. Until I know what we're dealing with on this one, I'll assume the worst, and haul everything I can think of with us. I'm afraid you're right about the summoning. It feels like it's tied to the castle, like Lance Corporal Jackson hinted at. The place looks totally abandoned and long forgotten, but now it's suddenly a danger. Something changed, and I have no idea what that might be. At least the description of our creatures having a tough hide rules out a few things. Poltergeists don't spark when you shoot them with a machine gun." Jones appreciated any little tidbit that would help him categorize what they faced. Besides, he hated even the idea of ghosts.

For everything he eliminated, he thought of three new possibilities. Jones slapped a hand on the top of the armored car. "Well, I've already got the equipment here. Not much point in going through the list of possibilities over and over if I can't do anything about it. We have a few pictures and a new report, but it sounds to me like there's not much new to learn here at the Aerodrome now that we have information on the castle. Nobody else is going in before us, so we're both forward observers and response team. I hope we have everything we need."

The good news was that in almost every case, the application of enough firepower would win the day. He'd had almost enough firepower on the last mission, and he'd still lost two men. He didn't want that to happen again, and he would go for extreme overkill whenever possible. Rabid enchanted squirrel? Explosives. Minor haunting of an abandoned manor? Burn that sucker to the ground, with prejudice. He wasn't in a mood to mess around. His men deserved his best efforts, and he wouldn't fail them again.

It was a good thing the men had only unpacked the bare necessities for their stop at the Aerodrome. Jones and his team ate a quick supper with the locals, then bid farewell to the pilot and bombardier. "Keep the tent set up and the radio turned on. We hope this is a quick mission, in and out."

Colonel Dubois watched from the doorway to the camp offices, scowling the whole time. Jones had pulled rank a second time with his letter to keep Lance Corporal Jackson and his French bombardier at the base, waiting by the radio for either news or orders, as Jones and his team took their Peugeot armored cars to the border and into Belgium. He had a stack of photographs for reference near the castle, and he reviewed his options as they drove off.

The two witnesses were a great resource, much better than that stuffy base commander. Jones would deal with the fallout later, since he'd added extra friction between the aviators and their commanding officer.

Despite the tension, the pilot was doubly useful, already knowing the roads and mountains the rifle squad planned to travel and warning them of several potential hazards along each possible path through the countryside. Some routes had impassible roads. The residents of some towns resented intrusions to the point of firing on anything military, no matter who it belonged to.

Jones saw vehicles parked beside the road in the distance, right on schedule, as they drew near to the border. "Private Harris, I think that's the border roadblock the pilot told us about. Are you ready to talk our way through again?" It was the third roadblock in less than an hour, but the first two had been happy to let the Americans through. As they approached, Jones made out men standing beside the road, and three more standing near their armored vehicles. A makeshift gate made up of two barrels and a long board stood across the road.

John M. Olsen

"As ready as I'll ever be, sir. They're supposed to be French, right?"

"That's right." Jones squinted through the windscreen in the late evening sunlight. "Yes, the uniforms match."

Harris pulled the lead car to a halt and leaned out the window to speak back and forth with two men at the gate. The exchange grew heated until Harris turned to Jones. "They say the road's closed. Nobody is allowed beyond the gate without approval, and I can't figure out who they expect the approval to be from."

Quiet enough not to be overheard by the gate guards, Jones replied, "We know that's a lie. They want something, but what? Food? Money? Lance Corporal Brown, take a look at their supplies. See what they've got crated up beside their trucks."

Word came back to the front seat from above as Brown scanned the area with binoculars. "I see plenty of weapons, ammunition, and general equipment. Not much food."

"Perfect. I know how to deal with this. It might delay our post-mission party until I can resupply, though." Jones squeezed into the back, found the box he was after, and pulled the lid loose. Inside were several luxuries he'd picked up over the past few months. At the conclusion of each mission, he pulled something at random from the box to liven the spirits of the team. He'd skipped the party box after the last trip, hoping to give the men some time to grieve.

Jones got out of the car and carried the small box around to the driver side, where Harris spoke with the gate guard. "Tell him this is our gift of appreciation as they work this terrible post so far away from the good things in life. It's nice to have friends at critical locations like this, and I want to think of them as our friends."

"The party box? If you're sure, sir." Harris relayed the message as Jones exposed the contents. Chocolate bars, a coffee can, and packs of cigarettes sat in tight bundles within the box. Lurking in the bottom of the box was a bottle of liquor. The guard's eyes grew wide, and he traded words back and forth again with Harris, who smiled and spoke in as friendly a tone as Jones had ever heard from him in their short time together.

The soldier turned to shout something back and forth with two of his friends, then turned back to Harris and nodded with a smile. The deal was done.

"Merci beaucoup," the soldier said finally, accepting the proffered box with a nod of the head. He raised his voice and called to his companions, who lifted the board from the barrels and cleared the path for them to proceed.

The boys would make a lot of noise about it later, but sometimes a carrot worked better than a stick. They continued on their way, entering Belgium. He could make up for the loss of the party box after they returned from the mission. A special night out on the town as a squad would improve their spirits, anyway.

The deeper they ventured into Belgium, the worse the roads got. "Didn't Jackson say this was the best road to where we're going?"

Harris glanced over as he replied, "Yes, sir. The others have been bombed and torn up a lot worse. The French don't want these roads being used to transport troops, but this one doesn't really lead to anything significant. Nothing but pastures and farmland up here."

The smell of smoke had come and gone several times as they drove through the countryside. "I can see why Jackson likes flying. No roads to deal with. Too bad he couldn't fly us in, drop us off, and save us a day of travel." He made a mental note to look into potential uses for biplanes within Special Unit 13. The idea of soaring overhead, looking down on the unmaintained roads had a huge appeal. A rough bump jolted him out of his thoughts. "What was that?"

The private muttered under his breath as he peered through the windscreen into the darkening sky. "Sorry, sir. I caught a bad rut in the dark. The roads might be less bombed, but they're less traveled here, too. Most are meant for horse-drawn wagons. We'll have to stop soon and pick back up in the morning."

"Find a wide spot or a field. We'll set up camp and check in via radio."

Soon, both vehicles sat side-by-side at the edge of a field of grain, still green and growing.

"I'm le tired after all that driving," said Lance Corporal Davis, using his fake French accent. Even Jones knew the language didn't work that way, but it did no good to correct or discourage Davis. Either reaction would get more bad French.

"Fireteam Two, I want the radio set up so we can call back to the Aerodrome. Fireteam One, set up a tent. Anderson and Davis, you're on watch, unless you're too tired and need your beauty sleep."

The men chuckled as they set about their assigned tasks with their usual precision and alacrity. This was an old, familiar drill, and before long they had a tidy camp ready for the evening.

On a map spread out on the hood of the Peugeot in front of the armored cab, Jones measured off the distances between towns with a small divider and narrowed down their position. A couple of compass sightings of nearby high points refined his estimate. He penciled an X on the map. They'd made good time despite the condition of the roads.

Private Robinson raised a hand from where he sat near the radio cabinet. "Sergeant, we got the Aerodrome."

Jones made his way to the radio. Moore, one of the men assigned to haul the radio, wore headphones and took notes as he occasionally spoke into a microphone. "Right at the branch, then another five miles. Got it. Then on foot. How many miles is that? Oh, that's not good. Hold on."

Moore tapped a pencil on his notepad. "Fifteen-mile hike from where the roads end. Do we really want to haul all this equipment that far on our backs, sir?"

Jones cursed under his breath. "What we want doesn't make any difference. The equipment goes with us, even if we have to abandon the vehicles. Ask them about locals. Horses and carts, maybe. Colonel Dubois may be more useful than I thought if he can tell us the best way to haul everything via pack animal, and where we might find some."

After a few moments of conversation, Moore sat back and set the headphones down. "They'll check with the colonel and get back to us soon. They didn't sound confident. I have info on a couple of nearby farms that may still be occupied."

"Harris, are you up for negotiating with some locals to get horses?"

"Yes, sir. Do we know which side the locals are likely to sympathize with? It could go either way here." Jones regretted giving away the entire party box. Locals would have appreciated the luxuries he'd given to the French soldiers at the checkpoint. He had money, but war had made the value of paper currency unpredictable, and you couldn't eat money.

Moore shrugged. "Allegiance could vary from one farm to the next. The pilot might know the terrain, but he only flies over it. He can't talk to the farmers."

If they were like typical civilians, Jones knew they'd enthusiastically support whatever side didn't shoot them or rob them blind—assuming they hadn't already been shot or robbed. Everyone liked to assume the enemy was depraved and did horrible things to innocent victims, but Jones knew enough about war to know there were bad apples on all sides of every conflict. "In the morning, we find a farm and go in to talk with them, just me and Harris. I want all the riflemen set up in sniper positions in case things go bad and we run into hidden opposition. We'll offer them a fair payment for what we need. Is everyone clear?"

An hour later, the fliers pulled through with intel on what sort of equipment to ask for to go with horses, and what the locals might consider a fair deal under the current threat of war. The price for such sturdy animals was high during wartime, but that was what expense reports were for. He wouldn't spend money unless he had to, but he wasn't afraid to offer up sacred government funds to get the job done. Money was a tool, just like any other at his disposal.

Jones and his men settled in for the night. Exhaustion showed on everyone's faces and in their posture after all the driving over rough roads, and tomorrow promised to be another long day of even harder travel.

Jones sat up front beside Private Harris as he had the day before. The team was back on the road in the early morning light before sunrise, and Jones directed Harris to take the branch recommended to them by the fliers back at the Aerodrome. "Are you ready to talk to the locals? We don't want to scare or threaten them."

"No problem, sir. I've got a good guess which Dutch dialect they might speak here, so I'll start off with that."

Another road rut jostled them, generating grunts and complaints from the men in the back of the vehicle. These dirt roads weren't a comfortable way to travel, but riding sure beat walking. Roads near the cities had improved noticeably over Jones' lifetime with the growing popularity of automobiles, but rural areas like this hadn't changed much from generations before.

A farmhouse came into view off to the side of the road, nestled back into an open field cleared of trees. Green pastures extended behind the house to a tree line. The road itself had become little more than dual tracks of dirt trampled into the grass. Jones was unsure if a motorized vehicle had ever been here before. A low stone wall surrounded the well-maintained house, a Tudor wood and stucco structure on a fieldstone foundation typical of much of Europe. Everything was still. No children or adults peeked out, and the doors of a barn behind the house swung in the light morning breeze.

"Fireteam One, get out and to the right. Two, go to the left. Stop here, Harris. Something's not right."

With the others in place to watch for trouble, Jones and Harris got out and made their way toward the house, nerves burning with anticipation. Their boots crunched as they walked the gravel path from the low wall to the door of the farmhouse. Jones pounded three times on the door, but got no response. Had they abandoned their farm to head somewhere safer? He tried the handle, and the door opened.

One glance inside was all he needed, as the smell of decay hit him in the face like a fist. He pulled the door closed.

"Aren't we going in to look around?" asked Harris from a few paces behind.

"I saw all I needed to see." Several flies buzzed around them, having escaped the house while the door was open. "We won't be talking to anyone here. Keep everyone out of the house for me, Private." If the mission went well, maybe he could take time later to return and dig graves for the family who lay bound and executed in their living room. Jones waved the teams in to meet in front of the farmhouse.

"This is about as far as we can drive. We'll be on foot from here to the old castle. Unload the equipment and get ready to march."

"Sir? Le horses." It was Davis again with his horrible pretend French, but he stood and pointed out beyond a pasture where two horses stood and grazed. Someone must have let them out before the family died. Jones glanced to the open barn door and pictured the horses being set free by a panicked farmer as soldiers arrived.

"Well, then. Who knows how to catch horses?" The men returned blank stares, except Corporal Anderson, who made a comment about city boys under his breath.

"I was raised on a farm, sir, but it's not a one-person job if they don't take a liking to me. They'll do whatever we want if we can make them think it's their idea."

"Fine. We do this with military methods. We set up a perimeter and get Anderson leading Fireteam Three behind them to drive them slowly forward while the rest of us steer them into the barn by constricting their path along the sides. Make the barn look like the easy way to escape, and they'll go that way. From there, see if there's grain or hay we can entice them with. Anderson, once we have them in the barn, I want you to take inventory. Lance Corporal Moore knows the equipment we were supposed to ask for. Find out if we have what we need. You have the lead, Anderson. Call out if you need us to move."

Within minutes, the horses stood inside the barn with docile expressions. If only every military operation ran so smoothly. The equipment for using the horses as pack animals left a lot to be desired, but Anderson got a makeshift pack saddle on each horse. It took a length of rope and a lot of creativity to get the radio—the heaviest of their gear—packed up to lighten Fireteam Two's load to more manageable levels.

When the two horses were ready to go, Jones had the men pull the vehicles into the barn to reduce the chance of them being stolen. To secure the scene, he had his men push an old, broken-down wagon in front of the barn door.

Soon they were on their way, with fifteen hard, trackless miles of forest ahead of them.

Game trails made much of the passage easier, but the paths didn't always run in the right direction through the hills and forest. Jones stopped several times to get a compass fix on their position and check their progress on his map. When the game trails didn't cooperate, he blazed a trail, and took the men up and down hills through light ground cover. It was a hard, exhausting hike with full gear on their backs and the additional equipment on the horses that also needed care along the way.

Anderson called out to get Jones' attention. "Sir, the horses need another stop to rest. Well, the rest of us do, too, but the horses are putting out a lot of effort and need to eat some real food. The grass here helps, but it won't keep them going forever." He patted the sack of oats he'd added to the pack saddles. "It shouldn't be too long a break."

"Fireteam One, watch the right side; Fireteam Two, you watch the left. Anderson and Davis are on horse duty."

Anderson pulled out the oats as Davis tied the lead lines to a tree.

Davis rubbed the nose of each horse. "I'll call you Le Whiney, and you Le Whinette."

Anderson rolled his eyes and filled two feed bags, one for each horse.

As the temporary camp grew quiet, the forest noises resumed around them. Birds called out and small animals rustled in the underbrush. The canopy of shade from the tall trees was a blessing on the rough hike.

Jones rechecked his map and wiped his face to keep from tasting salt, as sweat ran freely during the tiring hike. "We can still make it by nightfall if the undergrowth stays thin like Jackson and Moreau said."

After a short break, they resumed their march. Hours ticked by as they settled into a routine of hiking and resting. The men agreed it was good to rest the horses, but Jones' own pack grew heavier as the hours piled up, and he secretly appreciated the stops required by their animal companions.

The sun dropped below the horizon, leaving the sky a darkening mix of blues and purples as Jones spotted the castle through the trees. "I want a little distance between us and the castle. Let's set up camp on the far side of this small hill so we can keep an eye on it without being fully exposed."

The forest stood utterly silent around them. No birds, no animals, nothing but a gentle breeze tugging at the trees as they set up camp.

Morning came early, especially after the long hike Jones and his rifle squad had endured the previous day. The castle loomed against the morning sky on the far side of a hill as the team prepared for their day. Other than a few blisters, the team pulled through as they always did, with their normal efficiency and lack of complaints. Now it was time to get down to business. He had creatures to identify and neutralize, and two possible rescues.

Jones tossed the dregs of his morning coffee into their small campfire. "Everything by the book, boys. We're in hostile territory. We have a downed aircraft and an unknown enemy in the immediate area—probably supernatural—with forces from the Central Powers a few miles to the north. Stay on your toes. The airplane should be a quarter mile in that direction." He pointed to the southwest.

His team slunk forward, advancing from tree to tree in waves that never exposed more than one or two Marines at a time. They'd drilled this sort of advance enough that it happened naturally. So far, so good.

Soon, Corporal Miller called a halt with a raised fist and eased back to talk to Jones. "The wreckage is visible from the rise here. It seems to be clear of hostiles, but it's a great place to set an ambush if anyone suspects we're in the area."

"Right. Fan out to both sides. We can set up our own defensive line in case there's trouble."

No enemy soldiers or monsters met them. Everything remained absolutely quiet. Unnaturally quiet. Some military men felt a pang of disappointment when everything resolved peacefully, but Jones sighed in relief as he finally stood beside the airplane wreckage to survey the damage firsthand.

Flies buzzed around his head. The wind shifted, and the strong odor of death reached him. He brought his rifle up to the ready, having fought creatures who smelled even worse on previous missions. A dozen more steps, and he lowered his rifle. The American pilot of the crashed plane lay crumpled and torn, his uniform only recognizable by a few scraps that retained their original color. A structural beam from the airplane ran through his chest. He hadn't suffered a slow, lingering death. Despite that, his body showed multiple unexplained wounds, as if something with claws or teeth had ripped him apart. A British Webley Mk V service revolver lay nearby on the ground, all six .455 rounds fired. "One body, American. We'll need a tarp and shovels. Anyone see the Belgian observer?"

A chorus of negative answers greeted him.

"If this is the observer's pistol, he was alive after the crash. That means he's still on the rescue list. Look for boot prints. Broken branches. Signs of a campfire. Anything. He has to be here somewhere."

The squad came up with a few boot prints, but the only tracks into or out of the area were their own, as if the man had been spirited away. Jones removed his helmet and scratched his head. Nobody disappeared from a crash like that without help.

With the perimeter cleared, Jones knelt beside the ravaged form in the wreck and pulled back the shreds of his military jacket. There about his neck was a round identification tag with a name stamped on it. Lance Corporal Daniel Clark. He gently removed the tag and stored it in a pocket for safekeeping. Tonight, they could call in a report of one aviator killed in action and an observer still missing.

Corporal White stood over a few boot prints discovered at the crash site, preserved in a patch of dried mud. "What did he do, fly away?"

Red eyes, flying, and resistant to gunfire. The reports flashed through Jones' mind. Added to that, it was big enough to carry a man away without leaving tracks. He still had no idea what he was facing, but he knew enough to be worried.

Corporal White patted a hand on the downed airplane. "Sergeant, take a look at this wreckage. Not much of this damage came from the crash. It's like the airplane at the Aerodrome, but a lot worse."

The canvas of the small fuselage hung in tattered shreds, and the wood underneath showed marks from both claws and teeth. The markings were dense enough that it had either taken a long time or several creatures to do so much damage. His level of worry grew. "We've got some tough, aggressive creatures here. The officers up the chain made a good call when they chose to send us." The question running through his mind was whether they'd brought enough weaponry. There was no way to know for sure until he made a positive identification and engaged.

"Moore, fire up the Marconi when we're done here. Have the fliers at the Aerodrome send a telegram back home with the new details. It looks like we have a whole nest of large flying creatures." His gaze drifted to the nearby trees. "Hold on, what do we have here?"

The mossy trunk of a nearby tree bore recent scars, but it wasn't on the path the aircraft had taken to its crumpled resting spot. On closer inspection, he discovered a deformed lead round embedded in the tree, as if it had hit something else first to flatten it. There were also bits of stone embedded in the bark. Small bits of gray stone lay scattered on the forest floor as well—out of place, but easily missed.

Jones examined several nearby stones jutting from the ground and found no bullet impacts, and nothing showing the same grainy gray stone texture. He hated mysteries. Unknowns sent him digging for answers. The answer to what they faced eluded him.

The crash had torn through the low growth of ground cover and leaves, leaving bare dirt in a long patch. He knelt to inspect the dirt and found his best clue yet. The soft soil showed a large print, with three clawed toes to the front, and one to the rear. Finally, something solid to go on. "Moore, make sure you describe this print in the report. Maybe the eggheads can match it to something."

He moved on to another print closer to the airplane. Four toes with small claws, but showing a long foot with a heel, rather than a rear claw for grasping. "That's odd. This print's not the same as the other one." Both were obviously recent footprints in the cleared soil, but they had nothing in common. Both styles seemed to be rear feet, so it had to be two radically different creatures cooperating.

His focus moved from actual living, breathing cryptids that just happened to be rare, and he considered otherworldly options as much more likely. "You're going to have to encode this one since it's going through the men back at the Aerodrome. Add sorcery to the list as almost certain." He hated sorcery more than he hated mysteries, and this smacked of people messing with powers best left alone.

He knew he didn't have to tell his men to take inventory and check their equipment. They all knew their jobs, whether as riflemen, sappers, or grenadiers. "Miller, have your team dig a grave for Lance Corporal

Daniel Clark, Killed in Action. Anderson and Davis, you're on perimeter again."

"Oui, oui, sir."

Guarding kept the two men occupied and away from the grave, which would otherwise be a constant reminder of their lost teammates. He fingered the identification tag in his pocket. This soldier deserved to be remembered with full honors, despite his hurried burial.

Using the Marconi for orders gave Jones an amazing turnaround time. Rather than moving the whole team or sending a messenger all the way back to a telegraph station, updated orders arrived within minutes. Even so, nothing in the orders surprised Sergeant Jones. Investigate, neutralize, occupy, and report. His orders were short and to the point, as usual. The castle became their primary target as the only reasonable location for the creatures.

It made sense that there were no trails around the castle if the creatures flew. But if they'd somehow been summoned or created, where were the people? For that matter, where were the creatures?

He sat at the radio with Moore, who was wearing the headphones and speaking with the fliers back at the Aerodrome. There was one major difference in the orders coming back. Jones had proposed a plan with aviators added to the mix in a minor supporting role. He'd figured the brass would nix it, but they'd been allowed. The answer came back with several code words indicating it was a secret and independent mission, but it also confirmed heavy use of the fliers. Either someone back home had a screw loose and figured Jackson and Moreau already knew enough to be brought into the mission, or the two men had inserted themselves into the fight as they relayed messages. Jones guessed the latter. "Warn those two jokers again that if they want to help, they'll be bait, and we can't do much from the ground to keep them safe."

Moore nodded and passed the information along. At the end of the radio conversation, Moore said, "It takes over an hour to get here, and they're scheduled to take off after dusk. It'll be full night before they get here. Turns out it's not just them. They convinced another pilot and gunner to come along with them. I think they borrowed a little authority from the home office rather than checking with Colonel Dubois. I've got instructions from them for using red lamps for signals to indicate bombing targets. Moreau's supposed to be an expert at dropping bombs. He said he had something special to test, like he was a little kid fresh from the toy store. They also have a box of smaller bombs, and a supply of heavy darts, but the darts are best against open groups of footmen, and I don't see anyone on foot here besides us."

"Good to know." Jones tucked the information away, a resource to draw upon when needed. "I doubt I'll have any bombing targets picked out for them by the time they arrive. The only real target is the castle, and I have no reason to blow it up yet. Our best bet is for them to draw the creatures out so we can get eyes on them."

The nearly full moon rose an hour before sunset as he reviewed his options. The moonlight made for good night operations for his team. The tricky part was his timeline. Based on information from the flier reconnaissance, an enemy force to the north could arrive within a day or two if they ran straight south. A lack of roads might slow the enemy, but the forest thinned out in that direction as well, complicating the issue.

He'd learned long ago to always assume the worst, so every change became a pleasant gift. That meant assuming the forces from the Central Powers to the north would run right through his position and past the castle as soon as possible, so he had to plan with that in mind. That meant clearing and securing the castle tonight. Besides, they had a missing man, apparently taken hostage more than three days ago.

"Remember, everyone. The primary goal is to remove the threat through any means necessary. Beyond that, we can work to find and free the hostage, or figure out the cause of the incident. I know we don't normally get to those secondary goals, but this time I have a feeling the hostage is important. He's a trained observer and could have critical information for us."

Lance Corporal Wilson patted a large box they'd brought in on the horse. "I've got the explosives. Once we're sure the castle is clear, we can blow the whole place if we need to. I've compared the payload with the size of the castle, and we can do it, with the right placement."

"Le Boom," said Davis.

Jones shook his head. "Only if we know it will take out the threat. We don't want it moving to another location. I don't want to have to track it down all over again. We start out careful and scout out the situation here." Working too quickly caused a whole different set of problems than working too slowly. His job was to find a balance in the middle ground.

Team morale would improve if they could pull out a quick victory, but he had to keep them all in check as they searched. The extra work of searching had a two-fold benefit. It would guarantee the place was clear of friendlies, and it would help him learn what they were facing and how to kill it.

Orders

Lance Corporal Jackson shook his head as he reviewed the incoming and outgoing telegrams. "And here I thought *my* messages were devoid of juicy bits. Did you see this? Half code-words, and all boring."

Moreau shrugged. "What do you expect, Jackson? That they should talk of flying monsters in open telegraphs?"

"Well, I think I figured out enough to emphasize the part we can play in helping them."

"That is a dangerous game. You are not working with a temporary assignment to the French. They are your own forces. Marines like you."

"Yes, but they bought it." Jackson sat back in his seat at the radio console. It took up most of the table in their office.

Moreau said, "You lied to them."

"No, I didn't. I sent their reports and relayed the orders back to them, with just a little added to emphasize how we can be effective as air support. I don't know why their orders have such a high priority, but as long as they can override Colonel Dubois, I'll make use of it to assure they have what they need. We already know they need help against something that can fly, so I made it easier to get what they need by adding us to their list of resources. If they're a ground force up against something airborne, we have more experience and expertise than they do. They need our help, whether they realize it or not."

Moreau's voice took on a tone showing he knew exactly what Jackson had up his sleeve. "So, you volunteered both of us to give them whatever help they need. Just so you know, Petit and Durland overheard our discussions earlier and insist on being added to the mission. They will fly the Farman MF.11 beside us."

"We can't let them do that."

Moreau wagged a finger. "Unless you want them reporting your creative use of telegraph and radio to Colonel Dubois, you must allow them to join us. They were most insistent."

It had started out so simple. Volunteer to help where he knew they could be of assistance to his fellow Marines. But nothing stayed simple, especially when war was involved. "Fine. I'll send a message to Sergeant Jones that two airplanes are flying into Belgium to join them tonight."

The decision to insert himself and Moreau as part of the night mission hadn't come lightly. Jackson had weighed the costs and the benefits. He had more experience than the Marines did with the creatures, or whatever it was out there. He also had experience working from the air to support ground troops. It gave them more tools and a better chance for success.

After adding information to the relayed telegraphed status report, it had annoyed Jackson to see their role reduced to almost nothing by the incoming orders. It took a lot of creative interpretation and a few implications to get everything lined back up, but they were in.

"Here's to a successful mission. May we be more useful than bait." He raised an imaginary glass to Moreau.

The two airplanes sat side-by-side on the airfield with fuel and ammunition arriving for the tandem flight. Flight crews worked on each aircraft alongside the head mechanic who supervised both teams. The black-fingered man verified the state of both engines, then reviewed the repairs he'd made to the Avro 504. Both airplanes had seen quite a lot of use lately, and both had been worked on extensively by the head mechanic and his team.

Without the care and attention of the mechanic, the machines would have failed long ago.

Moreau translated for the mechanic. "He says the broken wood beams are as good as new. Everything was either replaced with new lumber or splinted. We are running about five pounds heavier than before because of the repairs."

Jackson grabbed the tail and worked the rudder back and forth. "Anything to watch out for back here?"

"No. The cables and hinges are new. You never want to patch a control line. He doesn't trust repairing such vital pieces."

The quality of the repairs gave Jackson more confidence the longer he inspected the airplane. The mechanic did excellent work.

In a few hours it would be his turn to take the airplane back into combat. "It looks like we're all set once we have fuel and ammunition loaded."

Moreau pointed to the supply cart. "And bombs. Do not forget the bombs."

"How could I forget? I told the Marines you'll have your special twenty-five-pounder on hand. The Farman will have a full load-out of bombs under its wings as well, just in case they give us a target."

The photographs hadn't shown anything but trackless forest and an abandoned castle at the attack site, but Jackson had long ago given up trying to predict how a mission would go once the chaos of combat entered the equation.

After sunset, the two aircraft took off by the light of the moon and set course for their rendezvous. The familiar corridor into Belgium passed beneath them on their way to lend whatever assistance they could to the Marines on the ground.

Contact

My Dearest Pearl,

I'm afraid I haven't always been completely honest with you about my work. I can't be. Such is the nature of the military. My missions haven't always been as safe as I've implied. Here I am sitting in the growing dark, ready to search an old, abandoned castle to see what we can discover. It may be empty, but it may not be. People need me and my squad. We're good at what we do, and our job isn't all made of reports and training exercises.

It's not that I've ever tried to mislead you. You know me better than that. I may have left out an important detail or two from time to time, since I don't want you to worry. The stress is bad for your condition. I do whatever I can to make sure my men and I are safe, but danger can't always be avoided as a Marine. Our job is to go where the trouble is and make it stop.

This mission has me concerned. There are still too many unknowns, and we're too far from support if something goes wrong. The good news is, we have some additional help flying in on biplanes. You should see them. They come in different sizes and shapes specialized for different tasks. Each type is good at different things. One I saw floats on the water like a boat. What will they think of next?

Please know that everything I do is for you. I want you to be safe and happy, and I want you to live in a world where evil is a distant and weak thing. That's why I'm here. You're my spiritual anchor and returning to you is my greatest and eternal goal.

The sunlight is fading, so I don't have any more time to write. Know that I have loved you from the day we met, and I will love you forever, no matter what.

With love forever and always,

Sgt. George Jones, USMC

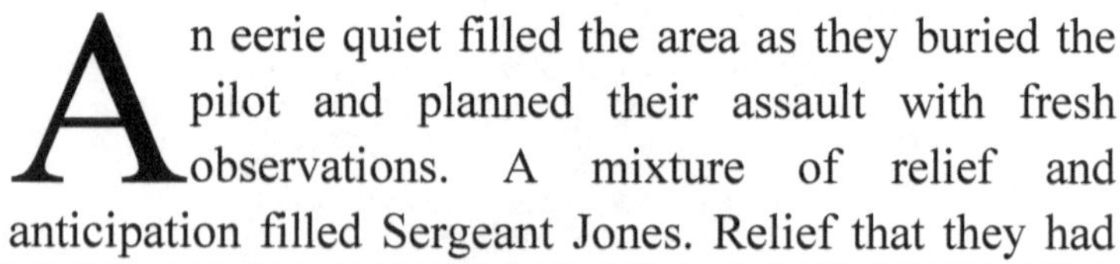

An eerie quiet filled the area as they buried the pilot and planned their assault with fresh observations. A mixture of relief and anticipation filled Sergeant Jones. Relief that they had uninterrupted time to plan, and anticipation to get to the meat of the mission. Plans were set, and the squad was as ready as they would ever be.

Night fell, and it was time to approach the castle. Peering through the open outer gate showed the castle's main doors also standing open, with enough gathered leaves piled up against them to show they hadn't closed in years. The lack of wildlife was noticeable, but not surprising. Many animals were sensitive to unnatural forces and avoided contact. And here Jones was, seeking out that unnatural contact. Squad members took turns napping during the day so they wouldn't begin the evening's combined assault already worn out from the day's efforts.

In the distance through the trees, Anderson settled the horses at their camp. It had done the beasts good to rest and graze the entire day after the work of hauling so much equipment with makeshift pack saddles. The tricky part now was for the animals to survive through the coming fight and carry the gear back out of the wilderness.

Jones checked his watch, then signaled Fireteams One and Two. "Miller, take your team to the left of the broken-down entrance. White, take your team to the right." He stayed back in the trees at the center position with the two men from Fireteam Three to cover the rear.

"Anderson, watch our backs and keep an eye on our camp. I don't want any surprises from that direction." It felt weird to have camp such a short distance away, with their stockpiled supplies within easy reach.

Despite their efforts to hide the site behind a hill, it wouldn't be too hard to find the camp if someone—or something—went searching. Anything able to fly could find their camp with next to no effort, but camping an hour away from what looked like an abandoned castle would eat up too much of their precious time in travel. He couldn't count on the camp remaining secret from the enemy, but Fireteam Three maintained the flexibility to keep an eye out and cover their backs as they maintained surveillance of the camp during the night mission.

The two assigned fireteams flanked the entrance, ready to spring into action on his command. Now they waited. Twice before, an airplane flying overhead had triggered an attack. If it happened a third time, they were in a great ambush location just outside the castle's courtyard wall, surrounded by enough trees to provide partial cover from the air. The trees and the wall also provided good cover against anything coming at them on the ground.

If everything went well during their foray into the castle to flush out and remove the threat, the aviators had a secondary task to get an updated position on the force from the Central Powers to the north. The earliest the aviators could report back on those findings was sometime in the morning. It wouldn't do at all to celebrate their mission success, only to discover the Kaiser's soldiers filling the forest all around them. Jones thrived under the pressure of deadlines, but he had to assume the enemy was on their way, whether it was true or not. He had to push his squad to complete their mission and leave before anything could complicate the mission further.

With Fireteam Three watching the camp behind him, Jones settled in to scan the sky between trees and wait for his nighttime air support to arrive.

The silence of the night changed gradually as a faint buzz grew in the air to the south. Jones tilted his head to listen to the sound of two airplane engines as they approached. The noise grew, but the airplanes remained hidden in the dark sky as they flew in from the Aerodrome. The trees on the gentle hills surrounding the castle ruined any chance of catching a glimpse of the airplanes, though the moon was out and providing enough light to see by.

Jones pulled out his flashlight and panned it across a visible section of the sky to the south, hoping to pinpoint their location to the aviators.

Another sound joined the background noise of the approaching airplanes; a grinding, scraping sound grew from inside the castle wall, echoing across the inner courtyard and out into the surrounding trees. Maybe that was the trick of it. With the noise coming from higher in the building, maybe his mystery creatures weren't watching from ground level. They would see the airplanes soon, just as they had twice before.

"Fireteam One, go." His command was barely loud enough to carry, but the team responded immediately, having been anxiously awaiting the order. The team moved through the gate to explore as the remainder of the squad held back as support. Fireteam Two sent one man around the wall to watch from the far side where he could monitor the progress of Fireteam One as they traversed the overgrown courtyard.

From his moonlit view through the missing gate, Jones saw the trees were less dense in the inner courtyard, but full-grown trees still grew wild and tall inside. This place hadn't been occupied for decades, perhaps centuries. At least by humans.

The airplanes grew louder overhead. Mixed with the grinding from the castle, it soon became impossible to relay commands to Fireteam Two without yelling across the space of the courtyard to where the men waited by the main door. The noise of stone on stone dropped to nothing. Suspicious of any change, Jones looked skyward in time to see several dark shapes silhouetted against the night sky, faintly illuminated by the nearly full moon. Each had a pair of glowing red eyes.

He counted nine shapes. Nine against the two airplanes were terrible odds. Turning to Fireteam One waiting at the outer gate, he yelled, "Watch the sky! Fire at anything that isn't our airplanes."

The time for stealth ended as gunfire and muzzle flashes erupted. His men spotted the winged shapes and sought to bring them down.

Each of the night-cloaked shapes from the castle bore two large bat-like wings, but they came in several shapes and sizes, no two seeming to be identical, as he'd seen with their footprints near the airplane wreckage. The different sizes still baffled him. Was there a purpose to it? Were they dealing with several types of flying creatures?

Having the creatures, whatever they were, away from their nesting spot was an opportunity he could use to his advantage. With the grinding noises quiet once more,

Jones called out to Fireteam One, "Miller, we need to finish our search for Mr. Laurens, and we need to get rid of this nest of creatures. Your team is up. Get in and begin your search, top down."

Behind Jones, Anderson appeared from the direction of camp and tagged Davis. "Loop to camp and back. We'll trade off."

"Oui, oui, Corporal Anderson." The American-accented French still grated on Jones, but he would let Davis have his fun, as long as he did his job. The man only knew about ten words of French, but got so much fun out of annoying the other team members with it that Jones let him keep it up. It especially grated on the linguist, Harris, so Jones generally kept the fireteams on different assignments, away from each other as much as possible.

Jones eyed Anderson, a well-practiced grenadier with a sharp eye. "Anderson, spot targets for me. I'm going to lend Fireteam Two a hand." Jones unslung his rifle and scanned the sky for more shadowy figures as occasional bursts of gunfire erupted from Fireteam Two's position at the gate in the wall.

"There! Two o'clock, forty-five degrees up," called Anderson.

Jones raised his Springfield bolt-action rifle and found a glint of moonlight illuminating wings. Five shots later, the shape dodged into cover behind a clump of tall trees.

"Maybe two hits, sir. Like the reports said, they spark on impact. At least one person from Fireteam Two hit the same one."

"If we can keep the airplanes from facing nine at once, the pilots might survive up there. Keep your eyes sharp and call out when you have a target." Jones replaced his magazine and chambered a new round.

Fireteam One entered the castle to search for enemies and hostages, while Fireteam Two made the best of their ambush as the creatures swarmed upward into the night sky from the castle. Aside from the creatures not using the wide-open front door, things ran according to plan. The number of creatures had also been a surprise, but he could scale up to deal with the increased threat. The search and rescue—combined with search and destroy— might all work out after all.

They could all make it out and go home this time.

Heavy fire from multiple rifles erupted again near the gate from Fireteam One. Jones glanced up in time to see a shape plummet from the sky in two pieces. A wing spiraled down separately from the creature. The form crashed through the trees, tearing branches off before it hit the ground with a palpable crunch that could be felt through the ground.

Jones watched the direction of fire from his team as he swung around toward the gate, waving for Anderson to follow him. He had to find out what they were fighting now that they had something to look at up close. A scratchy sound erupted from the trees, like the sound of rocks grinding together. That was the same sound the creatures had made before taking to the sky. Whether the sound came from movement or some attempt at speech was impossible to tell.

Concentrated fire erupted from the fireteam, then silence.

Jones skidded to a halt as half the team approached with rifles at the ready, coming in from two angles for a crossfire. Shredded leaves still drifted to the ground in the moonlight from where they'd been torn from the trees by the creature's rapid descent. More leaves settled to the forest floor in tatters from the gunfire.

The two men approached, then poked at it with bayonets that clanked and scraped along the creature's skin. Finally, they grew bolder and kicked it. The form didn't budge. Robinson, one of the two men investigating the downed enemy, said, "It's made of rock. How does rock fly?"

Pulling out his 1911 pistol, Jones announced his presence and joined them. The gray form sat on the ground with its head still raised in a frozen pose, its large mouth open to the sky. One front leg lay on the ground beside it, and the broken-off wing lay a few trees away, wedged tip-first into the ground where it had fallen. Observing the break where the wing had come off, the speckled granite surface ran all the way through as solid stone, just as Robinson had said.

Anderson came up behind him as Fireteam Two gathered and said, "A gargoyle? A real, live, flying gargoyle? I didn't know that was possible."

Jones reassessed the situation and scaled up the anticipated level of effort. "No wonder they're so tough. This explains the different footprints, too." Jones had seen things a lot weirder than flying monsters made of stone, but that didn't diminish the current situation. "Eyes up, men. The others are out there, and we know we can bring them down now. Anderson, pull your team in and spot for Fireteam Two. You still need to keep an eye on camp, so call out if you need to direct some firepower."

Jones had field research to do, despite the darkness. He retrieved a bulky flashlight and examined the stone corpse up close.

First, he noted that the downed creature hadn't changed position or moved since he arrived; a good sign it wasn't going to reassemble, come back to life, and attack again. After a fateful trip to Cairo, that was one of the first things he always checked. Its eyes no longer glowed, and they were a uniform part of the carved stone, as was every other piece he could find. No maker's mark showed on the stone as he examined the entire surface of the creature. With a little leverage, he turned it feet up to check for arcane marks underneath. Each foot bore a symbol.

Then Jones noticed its throat. The creature's mouth was still frozen halfway through a last, defiant howl that had sounded like chewed gravel. The throat was a dark reddish brown. Jones extended a finger and touched it, hoping the stone teeth wouldn't suddenly reanimate and bite off his hand. Something flaked off at his touch, so he picked at it and held the flakes up in the beam of his flashlight as he rubbed them between his fingers.

The flashlight spoiled his night vision, but this could be more important than shooting down another gargoyle. He sniffed at the residue, confirming his suspicion. Dried blood. A sure sign of sorcery, as if living stone turned into flying creatures wasn't indication enough.

He wasn't certain it had died due to losing a front leg, but the killing blow made sense after the examination. The wing bore no symbol, and the creature had frozen back into stone only after losing the front leg. Breaking one arcane symbol loose from the others had done the creature in.

It always felt better to know how to deal with a problem, even if it was a difficult problem. Blowing off a stone leg wasn't an easy thing to do, even with a good rifle. It was time to ramp things up.

Jones said, "Anderson, get back over here. I need you to run a message inside to Fireteam 1. You have to shoot an arm or leg off these things to stop them. While you're there, tell Martinez we're setting up his machine gun. Go."

Anderson sprinted off into the dark.

He could signal the airplanes to make a bombing run, but he had no target for them yet. His men were inside the castle, and no other bombing targets made any sense. This would stay primarily a ground operation for now, despite the rising and falling tones of aircraft engines in the night sky, and the occasional burst of gunfire from both ground and sky.

He strode to Corporal White and said, "The machine gun is in a crate beside the Marconi, but Martinez is still inside the castle. Get it mounted and ready to fire into the sky. The more firepower we can aim at these creatures, the better. We might be able to draw another one off the airplanes and get it close enough to neutralize it."

Martinez was the only light machine gunner, since they'd given up quite a bit of heavy equipment to haul the radio with them. It had disturbed the usual division of work between Fireteam One and Two to pack the radio in, but that came in as only a distant concern.

The grinding stone calls of the creatures echoed from time to time across the sky. Maybe it hadn't been such a good idea to trade out weapon space for the radio gear. The noise reminded him of predators on the hunt, and the enemy here had plenty of targets to choose from.

Distraction

The plan to lure the creatures out of the castle worked amazingly well, as several shapes launched into the night air. Destroying all the creatures as they appeared, had proven more troublesome. Jackson counted the shapes flapping up toward him and the second airplane as men on the ground fired on the shapes. One lone creature had nearly taken them down on his last nighttime visit, and now he had to dodge several at once.

At least the moon was out, and he could spot them better than during the moonless hours he'd encountered them before. He also had plenty of warning, and another plane to help. The benefits were few and far between, but he had to focus on them to keep from losing hope. The American pilot looked around to see if he could spot their companions in the Farman MF.11 he'd brought out to take pictures during the day.

A flash of tracer fire made the other aircraft easy to locate, several hundred yards away. With their swivel gun, they might have better luck hitting their targets, particularly the creatures chasing from the rear.

It felt good to be back in his Avro 504, despite the obvious patches and repairs still needing paint and polish. The machine flew, and he felt more comfortable in the airplane he'd spent most of his time in over the past several months. He dodged to the side as a shape appeared, then dove and lined up with a form circling its way up to his altitude. Moreau caught sight of it and fired the wing-mounted machine gun as Jackson worked to keep the airplane aligned as long as possible. The rattle of the gun died as shell casings dropped toward the ground far below. The form continued its loop, unfazed. They'd missed.

Maybe it was time to work more as a team. Jackson spotted a nearby creature and banked into a turn that made him a tempting target. The creature took the bait and swooped in from behind as Jackson lined up to run perpendicular to the other plane's path. The timing worked, and he cut across less than a second after the other plane passed, giving the rear-mounted gunner in the other plane as much to work with as possible.

Tracer fire erupted at the last moment in a wild spray that panned from side to side, barely missing Jackson and Moreau. The creature broke off, and Jackson lost it in the darkness. He could only spend so much time looking behind his airplane. The other gunner apparently hadn't trained enough in team tactics.

Jackson looped back around, keeping an eye out for the flying monsters already at his higher altitude. The greatest danger always took priority, even if the lower ones made better targets. An occasional glance to the ground told him the Marines hadn't set out any red lamps to flag a bombing target. Dropping bombs relied entirely on the ground troops for that part of the mission, since Jackson had no way to tell where the men were on the ground. The bombs were secondary to drawing the creatures out so the Marines could do their work.

Another flash of dim gray against the velvety black sky pulled his attention. Jackson lined up again, holding steady as Moreau fired the gun. Jackson steered to march the gun's tracer path into the flying thing and was rewarded with several bursts of sparks. He continued on a straight line in a limited dive to keep the creature lined up, while Moreau poured more rounds into the target.

The thing froze and spiraled downward. The flash of a spark from ground-based fire was all the warning Jackson got of another creature intersecting with his path from the left. He yanked back and right on the stick, and the shape missed by inches as it passed beneath his feet. Its clawed arms reached toward him and raked along the fuselage, tearing through the canvas as it passed below him. Its large gray wings resembled those of a bat. The creature flapped and banked behind them. The wings were not as terrifying as its face, with its fangs and glowing red eyes.

It looked like any other gargoyle he'd seen along many church rooftops, except it was alive and trying to kill him. Even in the dark, he was sure the image of malevolent, hate-filled eyes would stick with him forever. Seeking to replace the image with something else, Jackson scanned the sky, then looked below to either side, wagging the wings right and left for a better view. Nothing. It had to be somewhere nearby.

Hadn't Moreau told him about gargoyles perched on the roof edge of the castle? Dark shapes lined the old rooftop along the edge, fuzzy shapes in the photographs. Could this be them? If it was, he had a good estimate of their numbers, based on the picture. Information like that would help the Marines on the ground, but he couldn't tell them anything until he was back at the Aerodrome, where the radio sat. If they tracked down the beast he'd sent to the ground, maybe they'd learn the nature of the creatures as well.

Another burst of tracer fire pinned down the path of the other airplane and its target, so Jackson banked into a turn and sped off to support the other aircraft. Their gunner might not be great at teamwork, but Jackson could put Moreau in a great spot to do his part if the other aircraft had a gargoyle chasing it. He would also stay near the castle as long as he was useful, waiting for a signal from the ground. Several more bursts of gunfire spat from the Farman MF.11. Things weren't going well for the other airplane.

Stealth wasn't much of an option with the loud engine, but if the creatures were distracted by the MF.11, he might have a chance to surprise one. Jackson flew an intercept course, compensating as the other plane attempted to evade a growing number of enemies.

A flying creature had good altitude behind the MF.11. A dive took it right in behind the plane, a tactic he'd seen them use before. As he lined up with the attacker, he yelled to Moreau, "Light it up!"

Tracers flew past the MF.11's tail in bursts, then several bullets hit the creature as Jackson adjusted his path. Matching fire erupted from the rear-mounted swivel gun of the MF.11, and another creature dropped from the sky in pieces. The other gunner might not know team tactics, but his aim had improved.

Too late, Jackson saw two creatures swoop in from either side of his companion aircraft and flare their wings as they grabbed hold of the upper wing of the biplane to either side of the cockpit. One grabbed the pilot by the arm, struggling to pull him free, as the other tore a section of wing off the airplane and clawed its way closer to the gunner. The shredded wings failed, crumpling under the assault. The creatures fought to grab the men aboard the airplane as it spiraled toward the ground.

The darkness vanished in a brilliant flash, followed a staccato shock wave as the bombs on the airplane detonated in a rapid chain reaction. Jackson squinted against the glare.

Pieces of creature and flaming aircraft rained down onto the forest below, along with the remains of the two men, as the brilliance of the explosion faded. Would Moreau be brave enough to detonate his own bombs if it came to that, if there was no way to survive? Jackson blinked away tears, blaming the moisture on the bright flash and his ruined night vision.

With the realization that he was the only target left in the sky, he resolved to lead the creatures as far away as possible to give the Marines on the ground as much time as he could to do their jobs. He would meet an alternate objective at the same time by locating the Kaiser's forces nearby. Communication with a radio would make things much easier, if they could ever shrink the radios to fit inside an airplane. Maybe smaller radios or more powerful airplanes would exist in a future generation, but for now, he had to survive to report back.

Jackson banked to the north, hoping to spot some evening campfires as he mourned the loss of his Aerodrome companions. Four shadowed forms fell in line behind him, just as he'd hoped.

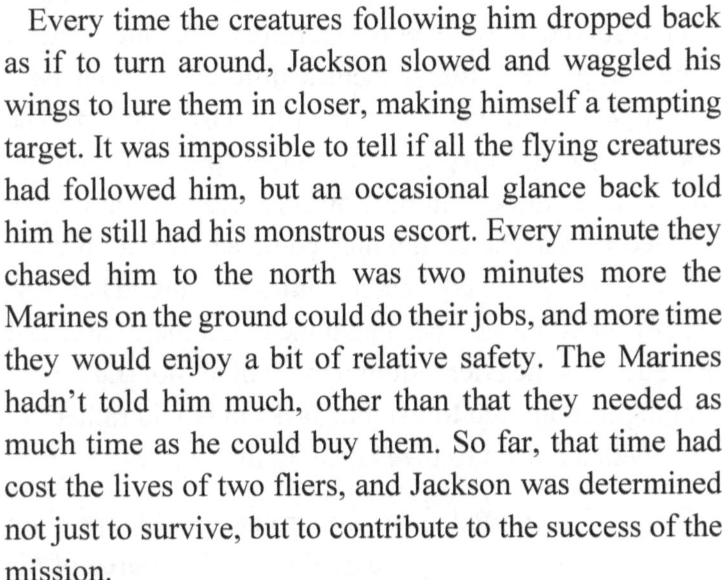

Every time the creatures following him dropped back as if to turn around, Jackson slowed and waggled his wings to lure them in closer, making himself a tempting target. It was impossible to tell if all the flying creatures had followed him, but an occasional glance back told him he still had his monstrous escort. Every minute they chased him to the north was two minutes more the Marines on the ground could do their jobs, and more time they would enjoy a bit of relative safety. The Marines hadn't told him much, other than that they needed as much time as he could buy them. So far, that time had cost the lives of two fliers, and Jackson was determined not just to survive, but to contribute to the success of the mission.

The Marines from the rifle squad were a secretive bunch, especially with the way they'd nearly taken over the telegraph office, to the point of sending and receiving their own messages rather than rely on the Aerodrome's telegraph operators. They were either an arrogant bunch, or they had connections a lot higher in the chain of command than Jackson's initial assumptions based on Sergeant Jones' rank. Jackson had no problem with competent men stepping in to get important things done, so long as they didn't pull others down as they did it. No, these men had experience taking control, getting important things done, then getting back out of the way.

Soon, Jackson saw a glimmer on the ground. The dim light resolved into several campfires, and then into a large camp. He'd found them a little closer than he'd hoped, several miles closer than his last sighting. The Marines had to hurry if they wanted to avoid scouting patrols from these Central Powers forces. If the enemy decided to visit the castle, they could easily march there on foot within a day, even with no roads. That was exactly what the Marines had done to get there. Some of the enemy's heavier equipment would not fare well running through the forest, but Jackson would rather not give them a reason to investigate to the south.

Tracer fire erupted from the ground, and a spotlight cast a beam into the sky, searching for the source of his engine noise. Then a second machine gun spewed tracers. Jackson banked into an evasive left and right turn, but the shots and spotlight had all been behind him. They missed him by a large margin.

Moreau turned around in his seat and looked over Jackson's shoulder with a confused look, then a grin blossomed on his face as he gave a hand signal to continue straight and level.

Straight and level with enemy guns firing into the sky? What craziness was the Frenchman up to now? If the spotlight landed on them, they had a good chance of being shot down. But like before, he trusted Moreau. Tracers continued to lance into the sky behind them, occasionally sparking off one of the flying forms. The Frenchman laughed and clapped at the scene behind them as guns on the ground fired into the flock of creatures following them.

Moreau rose to his feet and came up with a box. Surely, he wasn't going to use the much-needed bombs on the force below, was he?

With a sigh of relief, Jackson saw Moreau pull a handful of heavy iron darts from the box, and he gave the bombardier a thumbs-up sign.

Moreau looked over the side of the fuselage, leaning back past the wing to check their alignment with the camp below, then tossed the darts out two and three at a time until his box was empty.

There was no gratifying flash of light or explosion. The darts were meant for other purposes. Densely packed forces were the best targets for bombardment with darts, and the demoralizing effect of silent danger raining from the sky would force them to wear helmets constantly and might slow the force down with freshly wounded soldiers. From now on, the camp would wake at the sound of an airplane engine and scramble out of fear, even if it was an ally.

Finally, Moreau turned around, fastened his safety harness once more, and signaled for a sweeping turn that avoided a return path directly over the enemy forces on the ground.

Moreau leaned over the side to watch, then signaled some adjusting turns, letting Jackson focus on the sky above, keeping watch for any winged creatures that made it past the gunfire from the ground.

Yelling over the engine noise, Moreau said, "Deux! The army shot down two of the creatures. Luck is with us."

That was half of what he'd seen following them from the castle. His odds of surviving the night had gone up another notch. In contrast, he worried about the creatures that had just been shot down. If the enemy discovered the stone corpses of the gargoyles, their curiosity might demand that they send a group ahead on foot to investigate. The Marines would run out of time faster if the forces below him had reason to move, and he might have just given them a reason.

Perhaps his good luck would last, and they wouldn't investigate. And thinking of luck, how had the men on the ground missed his airplane so badly while aiming their spotlight? Everyone knew about the Doppler effect that caused an airplane's sound to arrive late, didn't they? All it would have taken was one spotlight operator leading the sound to point at the airplane itself, and the Avro 504 would've become the primary target instead of being missed.

Jackson counted his luck on that one. Once the spotlight found a gray-winged target, it stuck to it to help the ground gunners. That was the only explanation he could think of that made sense.

At least two more beasts had to be somewhere nearby still, but it was time to fly back to the castle to watch for signals. He wouldn't have a lot of time if he was going to make it all the way back to the Aerodrome on his limited fuel, but he'd do what he could for them. He hoped it was enough, as he sped ahead of the two creatures that still trailed behind him in a wide turn.

The two remaining gargoyles bothered Jackson. Not physically, but the idea of them following him had his mind racing to find a way to deal with them. If he took them back to the castle, where he had to constantly maneuver, the creatures would become an extra hazard, and who knew how many more creatures might still be at the castle? He formed and rejected several plans on how to handle them. Halfway back to the castle, Jackson yelled to Moreau, "I have a plan."

"For what?"

"The last two. I think we can kill them."

The creatures coordinated with each other, but not well, and only when they were close. Maybe they spoke to each other somehow. He'd seen enough of their flight patterns by now to see how they hunted in pairs, driving prey into one another as a team, but more often, they attacked solo. It was time to trick them into a fatal mistake. Cutting his throttle to minimum, he slowed, losing altitude as Moreau worked to spot the two followers. Within a minute Moreau signaled that he had both in sight behind them just above their own altitude. That would do.

Jackson slipped the throttle back up to its default setting and banked in a turn that would draw them off to the side, hoping to get a little distance between the two creatures. His first pass failed as the two stuck close together, but on the second pass, one broke off toward him, while the other hung back.

Rather than try to line them both up for the machine gun, Jackson came in from a perpendicular path with one creature on either side. "Fire a short burst!" He had to get their full attention and look like he was serious for his plan to work.

Moreau fired several rounds into the air between the two creatures, and they banked lazily to either side, well out of danger. The distance between them increased until they both wheeled around to close in from either side. Now came the tricky part. If splitting the path right between them didn't work, and the creatures were able to talk as they closed in, they might catch him despite his care and planning.

He cut the throttle as he compared their positions and speed with his own, then continued to close on a point right between the two, working for a three-way collision point. Moreau glanced back at Jackson with a look of panic, then from side to side as he tracked the two creatures. He wouldn't be able to hit either of them with the gun.

One of the creatures peeled off at the last moment, spoiling his plan as the airplane split the difference between the two creatures.

He had time for one more try. Turning back to the south, he kept his altitude the same, relying on their readiness to attack him over and over without tiring.

Moreau pointed out the gray glints as the creatures banked around to cut him off. Again, he balanced his speed with their approaches from the right and the left, cutting a path directly between them.

At the last moment, Jackson rammed the throttle to full, and hoped the creatures had paid close attention to his earlier maneuvers. Rather than pull up or to the side as he'd done over the castle and his last run past them, he dove moments before he would have caused a three-way impact.

The two creatures collided mere feet over Jackson's head with a resounding crash that threw rock splinters. The two creatures, both with claws out, had fallen victim to what Jackson had learned to avoid early in his piloting career. When he focused too much on his target, he lost track of other important details, like all the other aircraft in the sky. He knew men who'd crashed and died for no other reason than that they lost track of where the ground was after giving all their attention and focus to where an enemy plane flew. The gargoyles both wanted to catch him so badly that they'd failed to see each other until it was too late.

Moreau turned to watch as Jackson pulled out of his dive and banked back to fly toward the castle once more. Moreau leaned farther over the side and pantomimed spiraling down to the ground with his hands.

The trick wouldn't work when he had to pay attention to more than two, and it amazed him that the trick had worked even once, but the risk was worth the attempt to reduce the opponents over the castle. Now all he had to do was find the old structure again in the dark.

Summoner

More gargoyles appeared from the top of the castle and drove Jones and his men toward the central building, leaving them no room to maneuver, or even an easy path to get back to their campsite. They'd already had to move twice. "Everyone inside!" Jones yelled. "Fireteam One, cover us."

One man grabbed the overheated machine gun and cursed as it burned his hands. Jones grabbed it by the tripod and hefted it high onto his shoulder to keep the hot barrel away from his skin.

Another man carried a rifle by a strap only attached to the front of the gun, since a gargoyle had bitten the end of the rifle stock clean off during a lightning-fast trip through the gathered Marines outside the castle. If the creatures had wanted them all dead, they'd had all the opportunity they needed, and had chosen to pass it up. Jones filed the information away for later, after his men could regroup in a safer location. There was a reason behind everything, and he would find those reasons if he could. The creatures worked toward some unknown goal, and he could fight them more effectively if he understood that goal.

They scrambled away from the main gate into the courtyard and ran for the castle door as Fireteam One opened up to keep the flying creatures back.

Once everyone scrambled through the broken doorway, Jones followed and set up the gun to protect the narrow path through the large double doorway. Concentrated fire could keep the creatures at bay for a lot longer inside the doorway where only one at a time could approach. He fired off several rounds as one creature swooped through the trees of the courtyard.

"Welcome to the castle, Sarge," said Miller as he waved at the large entry behind him. The room contained a grand staircase that rose from the center of the room and split to either side halfway up to the second floor. A large hall ran deeper into the castle in the shadows behind the stairs. Despite the filth and wear of decades, the entry held a feel of opulence and grandeur with the sweeping woodwork of the staircase. The plaster hadn't survived quite so well as the wood, especially on the ceiling, where several holes gaped, showing the night sky.

The grating screeches of their flying tormentors ceased as the gargoyles broke off and flew for cover out of sight of the doorway.

Relief showed on every face surrounding him. Jones almost felt bad for ruining their sense of relief as he cursed at the tactics being used against his squad. "They wanted us inside the castle. They're herding us. Miller, what have you seen on the inside so far?"

"We haven't had time to explore in a lot of detail, sir. Based on our quick tour, the upper floors are empty, but there's a body in a large study down the main hall and to the left."

Jones peered through the doorway and into the moonlit courtyard. "Dead? You should lead with information like that. How long ago? Is it the Belgian observer?" Visions of locals out exploring the countryside for a place to hide from roving military forces filled his mind.

"Mummified. It's been here a long time."

"Ah, that's a lower priority, then." Relief filled his thoughts.

"Also, the room has books set out on a table."

Alarm bells went off in Jones' head. "Books? Remember how I just mentioned you should lead with the most crucial information? Show me. Harris, we might need a translator. Everyone else, keep an eye on the doorway into the courtyard, and don't assume it's safe behind you, either. The gargoyles pushed us inside on purpose, and I don't know why yet." Jones had never learned a second language, and relied on Harris, the newest member of his team, for local translations. Europe was funny that way. A single day of travel could put you in a different country where people spoke a different language, and not just a different dialect. French to German, German to Dutch. They spoke English just over the English Channel. Jones had traveled for a full day by train through Texas once, and hadn't even left the state, let alone changed countries, languages, or dialects.

Miller said, "In here, sir." Chagrined that he'd been caught with his mind wandering right after telling his men to pay attention, Jones peered inside and clicked on his flashlight.

The room connected to the main castle hall through large double doors with hinges rusted into place, holding the door mostly open.

He sat his flashlight on the table beside three old leather-bound books. The room had at one point been opulent in its design and furnishings. A chandelier hung from the high ceiling, but it wore a cloak of cobwebs and filth. Aged wood paneling lined the walls, and a taint of musty age permeated the room, filling every corner like the dirt that had accumulated throughout the castle from years of exposure to the elements.

"Miller, I'll keep Harris in here with me, if you don't mind." It always worked best to treat fireteams as a unit, issuing orders through the team leader. Otherwise, it bypassed the authority of the lead, who more often than not knew better what to do with his men. There were exceptions, but Jones tried to keep them to a minimum.

"No problem, sir. I'll be out with the rest of the team." Miller rejoined the crew in the multi-story entry.

Voices from the hall faded into the background as he checked the room for threats. A large fireplace could be a second path into the room if something was small enough to climb down the chimney. He'd seen impressive chimneys before, and with flying creatures above the castle, that threat became very real, indeed.

On a couch lay the old, dried corpse his men had found. Miller hadn't mentioned that the man was bound to the couch face up with his arms stretched out to the side. No animals had torn the man apart at his death, so he lay there in tattered clothing several generations out of date.

"Harris, take a look at the books. Careful, though. I don't want you reading the wrong thing and ending up with glowing red eyes. I'd hate to have to kill you." The warning was only half in jest. You never knew what you'd find with arcane writings, and the whole collection defaulted to being burned as soon as possible for the sake of safety.

Harris pulled up a dusty chair and sat at the table where he gently hefted the top book and opened the cover, as if afraid the book would come apart at his touch.

"This one is a journal. It's an old Dutch dialect, but I can read it." After a pause, he added, "I mean, it's safe to read, too. Oh, good. Dated journal entries. The last entry is from 1750, over a hundred and fifty years ago. It looks like that guy's been on that couch for a long time waiting to be discovered." He set the book aside and reached for the second in the stack, but jerked his hand back as a spark jumped from the book to his index finger.

Jones gestured toward the book, giving it a steely-eyed glare. "Probably not quite so safe to read. You took the training on that, didn't you?"

"Yes, sir." Harris opened it and flipped through the pages at a quick pace, as Jones remembered from his training years before. It helped to get an overview and a sense of what it might contain without dwelling on any one thing for long enough to internalize any of the art or text. This kid was a keeper. "Even flipping through that fast, the pictures in this one gives me the creeps. No pentagrams, at least. It's the manual for creating the creatures. Created, not summoned. Well, technically, the spirits animating them would probably be summoned. It's most likely a weird mix of demonology and golems."

Harris set the second book aside and picked up the last one, flipping it open more casually than he had the first two. Jones expected his team to act with more care, but he wasn't worried about damaging books he planned to burn, anyway. The biggest worry was over the potency of the magic.

"Oh, here we are. How he gave the creatures a set of orders when he made them."

Jones strode over to the fireplace and peered up the chimney to gauge the size of a creature that might slide down through the opening, and he smiled at the narrowness of the shaft. While inspecting it, he said, "It confirms he made them? Not summoned?"

"Right. Well, there was some summoning involved, but mostly to infuse the statues with a fake sort of life."

"You said something about orders. Can we change their orders? That might help us kill them."

Harris thumbed through the third book for a bit. "Sorry, sir. They take orders when they're made, and that's it. It says here that the orders must comply with a small number of specific rules. The creatures only come to life at night, and they're tied to a roosting spot. They can't choose to leave, but there's something weird about the phrasing here, and I'm not sure if I translated the roosting spot right. I'll have to noodle on this for a bit."

"Only at night? Great. We waited for nightfall before we approached, right when they came out to play. That timing could have worked out better. At least it explains why we didn't run into any when we inspected the airplane wreckage during the day."

Harris went back to the journal and flipped through the handwritten book before stopping on a page and poking it with a finger. "That's weird." He set the book down and walked over to inspect the dried corpse of the sorcerer.

"I just finished explaining to Miller that you put the important information up front. You should know better than to stop talking after saying 'that's weird.' It makes me nervous, Harris."

"It's just that he said he used his own blood to create four gargoyles, and it made him weak to lose so much blood. We saw lots more gargoyles than he accounts for in his notes. And look here." Harris indicated the wrists of the corpse. Old, stained shirt cuffs fell apart as he tugged on them to expose wrists slashed open, rather than the surgical precision he'd expect from someone providing blood voluntarily. "Oh, this is bad. He didn't make the rest of the creatures."

"But who would come in here, kill him, and finish his work?" A possibility tugged at the back of his mind, but he waited on Harris, as the private bounced between the book on orders and the journal.

Harris slapped the books closed and stepped back from the table to peer through the dark at the mummified remains of the sorcerer. He paced around the room twice with his hands laced behind his neck as he thought. "I think it was the gargoyles. We need to find out what orders he gave them. I'm pretty sure they killed him to make more, but to be able to do that, he would have to screw up his instructions to them pretty bad."

The gravity of the situation dawned on him as Jones considered the news. "But if they can make more of themselves, when do they stop?" His job had just become not only more difficult, but much more important. He had to destroy them to keep them from expanding into a stronger and stronger force.

Harris wandered back to the table and rested a hand protectively on the stack of books before opening the journal again.

"Here it is. Protect their home at all costs. That's one of the stupidest things he could have done. It's too open-ended. I could have come up with better orders than that. I don't know how smart the gargoyles are, but they have to be smart enough to understand orders. If they can understand orders, they can figure out how to interpret them in the most favorable way."

Jones barked out an unintentional laugh. "You mean it's like a story from a Thousand Arabian Nights? Give a genie a badly worded wish and he'll twist it back on you. It's the nature of evil to distort and corrupt everything it comes in contact with." That didn't make his job any easier, but it helped him to understand what they were up against.

A hundred-and-fifty-year-old stack of firewood and kindling sat beside the fireplace where it had collected dust in the study-turned-tomb. A chimney in use was less likely to be used against him, so he set a few logs out and cut some wood shavings to start a fire. It would give light to add to what the flashlights could provide.

As the firelight grew to provide flickering yellow light to the room, Jones talked through his options. "It might not be so bad. If we wait for them to go to sleep in the morning, we blow the whole building and call it a day."

"No good, sir. It says here that they're only vulnerable while awake. It says something about time stopping for them on the outside while they rest on the inside. It's like the creature and its perch become some sort of uber-stone during the day and can't be broken."

"Their perch? Like their home? What happens if we break or steal the perch while they're out flying around?" If he could fight them without facing the claws and teeth, all the better. After barely escaping the flying creatures outside, he was open to options, especially if it didn't risk the lives of his team. "Which book was that in?"

Harris closed the book and restacked the three tomes, lining them up with care. "It must have been in the one about giving them orders."

Harris pointed over to the corner of the room. "See that?"

Jones had his rifle aimed before realizing the corner was empty. Not quite empty, but at least not occupied by a killer creature made of stone. Sitting in the corner was an oval of granite covering a small section of the floor. "What am I looking at?"

"A perch."

"But they're gargoyles. Don't they live around the edges of the roof? They're waterspouts and decorations on the outside of the building." Jones pulled a folded photo from his pocket and pointed. "These dark spots along the roof are probably the gargoyles. That's their perches along the roof line."

Harris took his light over to inspect the stone oval. "No, see here? This is where the feet go during the day. There are two clean spots on this oval with no dust. The same sorcery must work with any kind of statue."

Jones knelt and inspected the thin stone platform, then wedged his bayonet between the platform and the checkerboard tiled floor. With a little effort, he got the blade underneath and lifted the stone up enough to get a hand under it. He hoisted it up to lean the oval against the wall, standing on its edge.

"What happens if I move this during the day while the creature is frozen on it?"

Harris, standing back by the books, cursed and slapped his forehead. "How could I be so stupid? I should have seen that. I missed it in my translating. They aren't locked to the castle. They're locked to the bases, and the bases can move."

The gargoyles couldn't relocate on their own, but they could be moved by someone else. There were instructions here in the books to create more, and they could be given fixed orders. If this got into Central Powers hands, it could change the war. For that matter, if it got into Allied hands, it could end the war sooner, but he'd sworn upon joining Special Unit 13 that he wouldn't allow such evil to exist, no matter whose hands it went to. Evil didn't care about good intentions, and would double back to corrupt and destroy anyone who tried to control it. He'd lost friends to the corrupting influence of evil and the power it promised.

His job wasn't to keep these abominations out of the hands of Central Powers. It went much farther than that. His job was to destroy them, along with anything related to creating them, via whatever tools he had on hand. Today, that meant guns, explosives, and fire. His standing orders were to destroy such unnatural things, no matter where, when, or how he ran across them, as soon as he could. Jones marched to the table and stacked the three books sitting in front of Harris, then picked them up and carried them to the fireplace.

"What are you doing, sir?"

"My job." Jones flipped the first book halfway open before tossing it open-side down into the growing fire within the hearth.

"No!" Harris jumped up and was halfway across the room when Jones tossed the others onto the fire and took up a defensive stance in front of the hearth with his rifle raised.

An anguished look came over Harris as he danced side to side and failed to find a path past his commanding officer to reach the hearth. "We could learn from those books. How to kill them. How to give them orders. How to make them stronger…"

"Stand down, Harris. You'll thank me later. I hope." Harris had already seen too much of the books, and it was a mercy to burn the texts before they could infect him further. The sergeant had one more reason to hate sorcery now. Even with extremely limited exposure, the evil had implanted itself and grown. That's why Special Unit 13 had rules, and now it was his turn to follow the rules and make sure this information died here. As it was, he would help the boys back home rewrite how to handle arcane texts based on this new information to destroy them at the first opportunity. Harris had followed all the safety instructions, and he'd still been influenced by the books.

Harris watched the fire as it consumed the books, his hands twitching at every pop and crackle of the burning leather and paper. His self-control held as Jones kept his steely eyes on the private until the books were well beyond any hope of rescue. A great flash of sparks flared up from the fire.

The private staggered backwards, then looked around. "Wow. The warnings in the training weren't nearly harsh enough. Sorry, sir. I think I need to sit for a bit. I'm just glad my eyes didn't glow red." He gave a meaningful look at the rifle Jones still held ready.

Jones let out a sigh of relief. He'd still have to make a special note in the kid's records about not exposing him to certain types of documents ever again. No sense in courting trouble. "Now, about this gargoyle perch." With a tiny push, Jones tipped the granite oval over, causing it to land flat with a bang like a rifle shot. It broke into several chunks with a brief flash of red light, making Harris jump.

"Well," said Jones, "that was easy."

Noise grew in the hallway outside as if the men dragged and rolled boulders across the stone floor. A mix of yells grew, with a keening howl in the background.

"If I'd read the books, I probably could have warned you about that." Harris gestured toward the hall.

"An acceptable trade-off, since I didn't have to shoot you." Jones rushed to the door to investigate the odd mix of sounds, popping around the door with his rifle aimed deeper into the castle toward the rumbling noise. From the hall he identified additional noises from outside, but much more muffled.

Men at the door to the courtyard took a couple of potshots outside and ducked back behind the cover of the door frame as other men crouched and aimed toward the interior noises. The gargoyles had them surrounded.

Martinez had his machine gun ready, but he aimed it up from its tripod as he gauged the threat, ready to fire in either direction as needed.

A stone face peered around the edge of a side passage deeper into the castle, and three rifles barked. The face pulled back to safety. Jones shouted, "Not until you can hit a limb! They won't die unless an arm or leg is gone." They had all heard those instructions before, but adrenaline did funny things to a Marine's memory in the heat of battle.

From the side passage where the creature had appeared, a faint voice transformed from wails to intelligible words, faint because of the distance. "Englishmen? Americans?"

Jones called out, "Mr. Laurens? Yes, we're Americans."

The voice returned after a moment. "Flee. Leave me. Quickly, before the runners climb the stairs. You made them angry. They will swarm you if you stay inside. You will die, or worse."

Jones stood at a moral crossroads. He'd fail at his secondary mission to rescue Mr. Laurens if he abandoned him. The man was a valuable resource in the war effort, and he knew more than anyone else about the castle, having been there for days now. In opposition, the spy trained to observe and analyze strategic situations had told him to abandon the rescue attempt, dooming himself to the gargoyles, probably to be bled to death to create more monsters.

A buzzing sound joined the growing din from outside. The airplane had returned.

In the space of a single moment, the choice became crystal clear. "Mr. Laurens, we will be back for you. Move out, men. We have an airplane to protect, and we need supplies from the camp." Like a crate of TNT.

Rescue

My Dearest Pearl,

Once again, I have just a minute or two to write. We're gathering supplies as we prepare to rescue a man. He told us to leave him behind, but I can't bring myself to leave him to a lingering death. The danger is increasing for my squad, but I can't leave him where he is and still have any claim to personal honor.

We were surprised by the dangers we found. The situation is more dire than I want to admit to the men. I didn't realize how tricky this mission would be, and I have to protect my squad while succeeding at our rescue without jeopardizing the original mission.

I have a plan, but so many things can go wrong. It's my job to hold everything together and keep the teams on track. They're good men, but if they see me waver, they might lose hope. At times, hope is all they have left.

Sometimes situations like this feel hopeless, but then I think of you and your emotional strength, and how you've always supported me, even when it was hard. Especially when it was hard. I remind myself that you're at home cheering for my success, and my hope flares back to life. It meant everything to me when you said in your last letter that you prayed for me every night and morning.

I'm blessed to have you as part of my life. I would die to keep you out of harm's way, but I prefer to fight for you today, and live to fight again tomorrow, so I can see you again and hold you in my arms. There's so much more I want to tell you, but I've run out of time once again. It's time for more fighting now.

With love forever and always,

Sgt. George Jones, USMC

Jones barked orders as the men converged on the camp. The gargoyles circled in confused patterns as if they weren't sure whether to attack the airplane or chase the retreating ground forces. Their confusion wouldn't last long if their past behavior held true. "Fireteam Two, get that radio running. Fireteam One, load up on ammo, and haul the crate of TNT to the castle.

Get every spare gun aimed at the sky on airplane watch. Shoot whatever you can to help our pilot survive up there. Fireteam Three, that leaves you to come up with a plan to distract the creatures inside the castle. We need the gargoyles—or whatever those runners are—out of the basement so we can get a team in there to pull Mr. Laurens out."

Davis puffed his chest out. "I am an expert at deception." At least the entire phrase was English, despite his attempt to make it sound French with his pronunciation of the last word.

Men scrambled to their tasks as Jones prowled through the camp and glanced up to the sky from time to time, keeping an eye out for stone predators. The creatures in the castle hadn't followed the squad out into the tree-filled grounds surrounding the castle. "Harris, tell everyone how the rules of engagement work with those things."

"Oh, right. Based on what I read, they follow strict rules, like unbreakable rules of engagement. Attack if one thing happens. Defend if another thing happens. Without knowing the exact rules, we can't predict new situations. Somehow, breaking the stone platform in the study triggered an extreme reaction, but only until we exited the castle. The indoor and outdoor varieties seem to interpret their orders differently based on their abilities, or they've divided up their jobs based on ability. The scary part is, they have a lot of freedom to learn new techniques to follow their rules. They won't react the same way again if they've learned something new."

The men grumbled at the news, but at least the ground-based creatures hadn't emerged from the castle to swarm the Marines. Without knowing the exact rules, Jones would have to improvise and make assumptions, and switch up tactics to keep the creatures off balance.

"The radio is hot, sir," Moore said as he monitored the gauges and switches on the Marconi.

"Tell whoever's manning it to get Colonel Dubois."

Two men set the crate of TNT at the edge of camp closest to the castle for easy access. The remaining machine gun ammunition appeared beside Martinez as he swiveled his gun around on its tripod and sent an occasional burst into the sky. During a pause, Martinez said, "The airplane must be running low on ammunition by now, but he's using his tracers to show me where the monsters are. He points, and I blast them. We make a good team."

A scream rang out as a stone-winged creature snatched Lance Corporal Brown from beside the TNT crate and hauled him into the sky after gliding in silently between the trees. Nobody could fire at the gargoyle without a high risk of hitting Brown as the creature worked to gain altitude.

As it beat its wings and passed the tops of the trees into the open sky, four rapid gunshots rang out. Brown and the gargoyle arced up for a moment, then plummeted through the trees to crash into the ground.

Jones and Fireteam One converged on the landing site to find Brown gasping for breath with blood on his lips. He held his 1911 pistol to the sky and croaked, "Got him. Blew his back leg clean off."

Brown lay underneath the stone gargoyle corpse, his body a crushed mess from the waist down underneath the carved stone. He laughed, but it turned into a choking cough as he labored to breathe. The stone arms of the creature still encircled him. The force of the landing had left shattered pelvis and femur fragments exposed where his body showed underneath the creature. Blood pooled on the surrounding ground.

Jones knelt beside him and gripped his shoulder. "You got him, all right. Hold tight and we'll take care of you. You're going to be right as rain in no time. You'll see."

"Everything hurts, Sarge. I…don't think I'm going to make it."

"Nonsense," said Jones as calmly as he could. "I've seen you come back worse than this from a night of heavy drinking. Everything will be fine." He squeezed Brown's free hand.

Lance Corporal William Brown, USMC, coughed again, marking Jones' uniform with a spray of red. He breathed his last, and his head lolled to the side. The pistol slipped from his fingers to rest on the forest floor.

Jones gently closed the dead man's eyes, retrieved the sidearm, then stood with his jaw clenched as he flipped the safety on and tucked the pistol into his belt for safekeeping. "We're going to rescue Mr. Laurens. We're going to destroy the gargoyles, every last one of them, inside and outside. Then we'll blow that castle to smithereens to prevent any chance of this mess falling into enemy hands."

He didn't have all the details worked out yet, but he had a squad of experts to help him, and together they would destroy the place or die trying. Of that, he was sure.

Within minutes, Moore called out from where he sat in front of the Marconi. "Got the colonel on the radio, sir. They woke him up."

Jones sat beside the radio where he could speak into the microphone, and he put on his best politicking voice. "Good evening, sir. We have a situation and require any and all assistance you can render with additional air support."

A voice crackled from the headphones. "You woke me to ask for more help? A sign of poor planning, indeed. What of the two *avions* already there? Have you lost them already?"

"No, sir. One aircraft was swarmed by the enemy and destroyed. The other is overhead now." Jones hated how the French colonel had put him on the defensive. If he only understood the gravity of the situation and what was at stake, Jones wouldn't have to dance through the polite request and play nice with the archaic cavalry leader. "Without additional support, we may not be able to achieve our objectives. Mr. Laurens is alive, and we are planning his rescue now."

"The answer is still no. You have cost me too much already. Equipment and lives are gone, and you call only because you also fail. I will lose no more."

John M. Olsen

Jones' voice grew calm despite the bulging veins in his neck. "Sir, this effort is more critical than you can know."

"Americans. All the same. All fools when it comes to fighting. So sure of their importance. My decision stands. There is nothing you can say to sway me."

"In that case, *sir*, I will do my best to see that you are court-martialed and stripped of rank for dereliction of duty for abandoning both your own forces and Allied forces when you had both the opportunity to help and a desperate request to provide aid. And if I'm very lucky, sir, I'll see you tied to a pole, where I will personally beat you for each dead man you might have saved. Then I hope to see you buried to your neck near the front lines, where you have a clear view of the trenches occupied by the Central Powers. If I recall correctly, those are all within the realm of possibility within the French Foreign Legion, are they not?"

"How dare you soil the name of the Foreign Legion!"

"I'm afraid it is you who soils their name with your lack of motivation, and not me. Good night, sir."

Jones set aside the headphones. "We're done with the radio. Thank you, Lance Corporal Moore." He pulled Brown's 1911 pistol from his belt and emptied its remaining rounds into the body of the radio, sending wood chips and bits of glass radio tube flying through the camp. "We can't let such a nice radio fall into the hands of the Central Powers, and when we move, we'll have to hurry. Now, back to business."

The men stood in stunned silence.

"I said back to business. We have a man to rescue, an airplane to protect, and a castle to destroy. Move."

A burst of gunfire from above broke them out of their trance. Martinez followed up with a few rounds at the target the airplane had just illuminated with tracers, grazing it as the creature flew overhead. The squad hurried about their assignments.

Jones listened as the two men of Fireteam Three explained their plan for a diversion. Davis held up a handful of large firecrackers, along with a length of rope. "I snuck these into my pack in case I had a good chance for le big surprise. Or, you know, to have a little fun after the mission. Did you know you can get these to detonate by tying them to a car's exhaust?" When Jones had considered the wide expertise of his rifle squad, he hadn't anticipated it including pranks.

Anderson joined the conversation. "See, we set up some noise on the top floor, but we wait to set it off. Then we head to a window, where we've strung an escape rope out to the perimeter wall. We pull down stacks of furniture on the top floor with ropes and toss in the fireworks as we leave the building, drawing the creatures up to the top of the castle, away from you on the main floor. Simple."

Jones wouldn't have described the convoluted plan as simple, but the idea did show promise. When they'd destroyed the one platform in the library, the gargoyles inside had become aggressive, right before Laurens had warned them to flee. Jones would rely on the gargoyles staying aggressive inside the castle to pull them out of the basement. Then there were the other aspects of the plan.

"Fireteam One, what have you got?"

Miller spoke for his team. "Brown was demolitions, rest his soul, but we've got his TNT and detonation equipment, along with some help from Moore with the charge placement. We'll set it up against one of the interior load-bearing walls, run wires out to our detonator just past the main gate, and then wait for your signal." The thoughtful consideration for Brown showed why the men had given him the nickname Brother Miller.

He had a big heart, but when it came to leading his fireteam, he was second to none at getting the job done.

"Good. And Fireteam Two?"

White said, "Once the explosives are in place and the diversion draws the creatures out of the basement and into the upper structure, we extract Mr. Laurens and take him to the rendezvous point, our camp."

Davis chuckled and broke out his ridiculous accent again. "You said rendezvous. Zat's French."

Jones scowled at him. "Davis, get your ropes ready and stop goofing around. See if Anderson needs help with his explosive charges."

"Oui oui, Sergeant Jones."

"Remember, everyone," Jones said, "Stealthy. Martinez, you're part of the distraction. Stay out here and keep shooting. Don't let them surprise you and keep your back to the wall." He left the rest unspoken—*Don't die like Brown did.*

The team eased in through the gate and past the large entry doors, moving more quietly than before. Anderson and Davis crept up the grand staircase for their job in the upper reaches of the castle, while Fireteam One placed the case of TNT at the base of a large support column toward the center of the main hall just past the stairs.

Jones left them to roll out a spool of wire, running it outside to the detonator by the gate in the exterior wall. It had to all be ready before the planned distraction upstairs. Martinez fulfilled his role outside, firing into the sky in short bursts.

Soon, all the pieces of the diversion and rescue mission were in place, with Anderson and Davis peering over the balcony as they waited for a signal. The explosives team gave a thumbs up, and Jones gave a go signal to the balcony, and to the team running back outside with the wiring. He hunkered down in an alcove with Fireteam Two to wait for the basement to empty. Everyone was out of sight.

Then chaos struck, right on schedule. From the top floor of the castle came the sound of an explosion, followed by a crashing and clanging, as if a dozen large pots and pans bounced across a stone floor all at once. The noise continued for several seconds as the sergeant wondered if the cookware would reach the grand staircase to tumble down. Just as he thought the noise was about to die off to nothing, another series began on the top floor. Sometimes Davis acted like an idiot, but there were no bounds to his creativity when Jones left him unsupervised to do things his own way.

A dozen dark shapes bounded through the main floor on a mix of two and four legs as they emerged from the hall leading to the basement. Some gargoyles were in the form of human-shaped statues and looked almost normal in the moonlight that filtered into the hall, but the process of animation had twisted each in some way, and they all had a look of wrongness about them in the way they moved. Their glowing red eyes caused shivers to run along the hairs standing up on Jones' neck. All but the last four-legged creature raced up the grand staircase two and three steps at a time as they sought out the source of the noise. One four-legged creature remained, sniffing at the wires running across the checkered floor of the large hall as it walked along the length of the wire. A small explosion went off to begin another cacophony in the upper reaches of the castle. With a final look around, the creature bounded up the stairs to join the others in their hunt.

Jones stepped out of the shadows and waved Fireteam One forward into the depths of the castle. This was their chance to search for Mr. Laurens.

The corner where he'd seen a stone face turned out to be the top of a staircase leading down. Jones and his team crept down the stairs, going by feel into the total darkness after a short distance. No glowing eyes appeared.

Once Jones and his team reached the base of the curved stairs, they flipped on their lights to search. A trail of fresh blood splatters and drag marks led them to the far corner of the lower level, where a man in his early thirties lay wearing a bloodstained shirt and filthy trousers. He held a rag to an injured arm. "I told you to leave me. You are fools."

"Mr. Laurens, you're not the first person to disagree with me tonight. You might not be the last, either, if I can help it. Can you stand?"

The man struggled to his knees, but fell back against the wall with a shake of his head. "Too much blood loss, and my knee is injured. They kept coming back for more blood, never killing me." Jones understood the need for fresh blood in creating new gargoyles, but didn't have time to explain. Two Marines helped the gargoyles' prisoner to stand, each draping one of the man's arms over a shoulder to hold him steady.

Looking around, Jones saw no stone platforms like the one he'd broken. "Do any of them stay down here with you during the day?"

"No, they all go up to the main floor or higher during the daytime." Mr. Laurens stifled a cough, trying to keep the noise to a minimum.

Jones pointed toward the ceiling. "Our distraction up there won't last long. Time to move. We go out fast and quiet, just like we came in."

They doused their lights on the stairs to the main floor, relying on feel to make their way up as they had on the way down. His fingers ran along the cool stone of the wall as they climbed one careful step at a time, finally emerging back onto the main floor.

Dim shadows from the indirect moonlight shone through the doorway, along with a hint of light from a handful of small windows.

Movement caught Jones' eye as they approached the grand stair. One of the creatures crept down the steps, silent as the shadows surrounding it.

From upstairs, a new noise arose. Davis yelled and cursed, running through every foul epithet Jones had ever heard, and then some in languages Jones didn't recognize. Leave it to Davis to learn nothing but profanity in foreign languages. He taunted, banged on things, and made a target of himself in the upper reaches of the castle. Despite all that, the creature on the stairs no more than glanced up before continuing to stalk down the stairs.

If these creatures were smart enough to divide targets and use tactics and strategy, it was time to change his own tactics. Jones raised his rifle and signaled his men to do the same. Just loud enough for his men to hear, he counted down. "Front legs. Three, two, one, fire."

They all opened up at once, each firing multiple rounds as the creature sprang into action and leapt down the remaining stairs. It charged across the floor toward Jones and his men. The Marines scattered for cover, but Mr. Laurens shrugged out of the grip of the two who held him upright and placed himself in the path of the creature. "They kept me alive before. They might still."

The gargoyle took an extra moment to dodge around Mr. Laurens as it closed on the Marines, and that was all Jones needed to aim in the near darkness. He fired three more shots from his rifle, emptying the magazine, as the creature charged. It screeched across the floor as a foreleg blew off in a shower of stone fragments. The now-frozen sculpture slammed into Jones, pinning him to the wall.

His men pulled the statue back, freeing him. Corporal Miller asked, "Do you need a hand, sir?"

He'd felt a pop at the impact, and his ribs flared with pain. "Just bruises. Let's go before more gargoyles come down the stairs. Keep an eye out behind us."

They retrieved Mr. Laurens and retreated as fast as they could out the front door.

Jones gasped at each breath, wondering if one of those bruises was a broken rib. Between painful breaths, he told Miller, "Call an all-clear for the basement. We need to get Fireteam Three out of there."

Miller bellowed out, "Basement is clear! Anderson and Davis, get out here!"

Out in the courtyard, Corporal Anderson waved. "I'm already out. Davis was right behind me, but he turned around and ran back in, saying something about needing to taunt them some more to keep everyone safe. He's lost his marbles in there. I should have made him go first." He stood, looking up to a third-floor window high on the castle wall. A rope ran at a slope from the window down to a tree growing next to the outer wall surrounding the courtyard. Davis waved from the window, then tipped an oval piece of stonework out through the window to crash on the ground in a dim flash of red light. He'd found another gargoyle pedestal.

Shrieks arose from within the castle as Davis let himself out to dangle from the rope, moving hand-over-hand toward the outer wall at a snail's pace. When he'd made it ten feet out, a creature appeared at the window, growling with a sound like a rolling barrel of rocks.

Jones called out, "Everyone, cover Davis! Hit the window he came out of." He slammed a new magazine into his rifle by feel in the dark as more shots rang out around him.

The creature, a skinny one resembling a man more than a typical gargoyle, made its way out to loop its hands over the line. Even the creatures made from statues had claws, fangs, and glowing eyes. Its narrow waist made it look as if it hadn't eaten in weeks. It slid along the sloped rope, picking up speed. With stone hands, it wouldn't suffer from rope burns from friction as its hands slid along the angled path.

A burst of machine gun fire came from the outer gate, and the lower half of the creature shed splinters of rock. Jones concentrated his fire on the same spot, hoping to hit the creature in a weakened area as it accelerated toward Davis, who hung only a few more feet down the rope.

Another burst of automatic fire, and the lower legs of the gargoyle dropped off. It died, frozen back into stone as the top half slid down the rope with increasing speed. Davis made a grab for it and missed as it hit him. He tumbled head over heels to the ground twenty feet below and crashed into the light undergrowth. Jones didn't know if he'd survived the fall until Davis continued uttering the string of curses he'd begun in the window, insulting the parentage, intelligence, and mating habits of the attacking creatures in several languages as he lay on his back, gasping for breath.

It took only a moment to reach him and offer a hand up. "Are you going to make it, Davis?"

He rubbed a fresh abrasion on his elbow and grimaced as he took an experimental breath. "Oui, Mon Sergeant." If he was back to butchering French, he couldn't be too bad off, aside from having the wind knocked out of him. Davis pulled himself up, and Jones locked his teeth together to keep from screaming as his ribs ground together at the effort. Definitely broken.

Jones found Miller from Fireteam One by following the wire running across the courtyard. "Got that detonator set up yet? The creatures are all upstairs, and this is our chance. If we collapse the whole building while they're away from their perches, we might stop them all in one shot. It won't matter whether we break the perches, or just keep them from going home to roost. They'll die either way, based on what Harris learned."

"Ten more seconds and we'll have the plunger hooked up. Everyone, get outside the wall." Miller waved everyone through the arch out of the courtyard and into the forest beyond like a hen gathering chicks. "Behind the wall should be safe enough. Maybe. The TNT is enough to take out that central support and bring all the walls down."

The moon hung low in the sky, but it still gave enough light to see by. Jones found Martinez manning his machine gun. "Do you have a count on remaining enemy fliers?"

"I'm not sure, sir. Some are still out there, but they're getting cautious. We took another one down. The airplane still has to dodge them, but I think he's figured them out well enough to keep them from sneaking up behind him."

Miller called out, "Martinez, time to fall back behind the wall. I don't want any friendly fire incidents with this TNT."

Martinez hoisted his tripod-mounted gun from the gate and set it back behind the wall as Harris dragged the ammunition box.

With everyone clear, Jones gave the signal to set off the crate of TNT. Miller pushed the plunger hooked to the wires, and nothing happened. He raised the bar and pressed it home with even more force, and still nothing.

Davis said, "What happened to le boom?"

Lance Corporal Moore, the only remaining sapper in the whole squad, squatted beside Miller. "Let me check the contacts." He disconnected the plunger and checked that it produced voltage. Next, he reattached the wires and declared the setup to be functional. "Something must be wrong with the wires. The detonator here looks fine."

"We have to go back in." Jones hated the thought of the extra risk, but there was no choice. The airplane had a few bombs, but not enough to guarantee the whole structure collapsed. He couldn't rely on the airplane to destroy the creatures and their home. "I need a sapper."

Corporal White gave Jones a sideways glance. "Why are you going back in, sir? I can take Moore with me to check out the wiring." That was as close as the man had ever come to questioning an order. It bore about as much weight as calling Jones an idiot for his misguided chivalry.

"Sorry, I need you and the rest of the squad out here covering my back." While the statement was true, it masked a deeper reason; Jones considered himself to be more expendable, especially with his damaged ribs. "I'm not going to send men somewhere I'm not willing to go myself. Moore, you're with me. There's no time for discussion." Despite the clear violation of protocol, White nodded, and Moore stepped up to enter the castle once again.

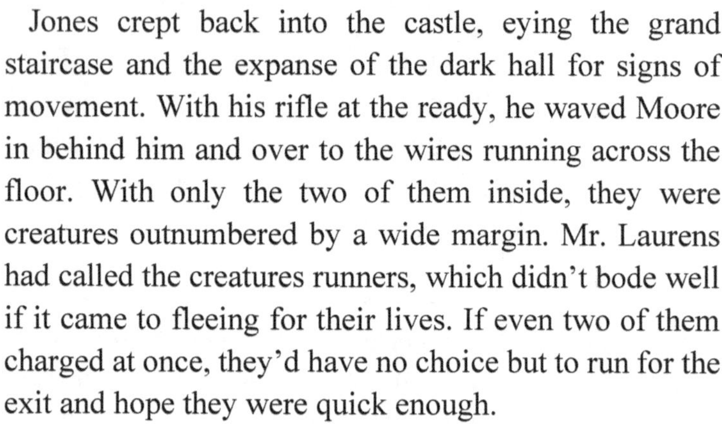

Jones crept back into the castle, eying the grand staircase and the expanse of the dark hall for signs of movement. With his rifle at the ready, he waved Moore in behind him and over to the wires running across the floor. With only the two of them inside, they were creatures outnumbered by a wide margin. Mr. Laurens had called the creatures runners, which didn't bode well if it came to fleeing for their lives. If even two of them charged at once, they'd have no choice but to run for the exit and hope they were quick enough.

The team outside already had their hands full with the remaining creatures in the air and taking care of injuries. Occasional bursts of gunfire from the air and the ground contrasted with the grave-like silence inside the castle. Every echo made Jones wince as he watched for the attack, he assumed would arrive any moment. He hadn't lived through so many bizarre missions by being careless, but any misstep could be his last.

What were the creatures trying to do? If he understood them, he could predict them. At first, the flying creatures had driven them indoors, where the other creatures were waiting in the basement. That resembled a cattle drive more than anything. The Marines had played the part of the cattle, but the gargoyles had discovered that their cattle had teeth. The Marines proved themselves to be a difficult target. That had driven a change in tactics, and the gargoyles had become much more defensive, except when a stone platform or perch was broken.

He thought he was on the verge of understanding their motives, but all he needed right now was enough time for Moore to fix the wires and get out.

If he failed, how many gargoyles could be made with the blood of nearly a dozen men? Then with more gargoyles, they'd use their additional numbers to overcome whoever visited the castle next, providing even more gargoyles to fight whoever stumbled across the castle in the future. Jones and his men had destroyed several of the creatures, and Jackson had done the same with his airplane, getting rid of a few more. The lost aviator had taken out more gargoyles when his airplane had exploded. Still, if it came down to an all-out coordinated assault, he and his men would lose. They weren't fast enough or accurate enough, especially in the dark. He hoped the gargoyles didn't realize that, or he and his men were doomed.

The explosives were the answer to his problem. All he had to do was destroy or bury their home bases and keep them away from their perches until morning. Any he could catch in the blast from the TNT would also drop from his list of problems. He was so close to a solution he could taste it, yet victory danced just out of his reach, taunting him.

A flash of tracers raced through a small patch of sky showing through a hole in the decaying roof above the entryway. Once the airplane ran out of ammunition, the air crew would have no defense against the flying gargoyles. He wouldn't lose a second flying team if he could help it.

Moore got up from his hands and knees beside the TNT and crept back to Jones, nodding toward the door into the courtyard. They eased out into the grasses outside. Moore spoke in hushed tones. "The wires in there are a mess. They've been crushed."

The creature that had come down the grand staircase was the most likely explanation. "I saw the thing walk along the wires. It must have ground right through them with its weight." How the heavy things were even able to fly was best answered by one of the most aggravating phrases Jones knew. It was magic.

Whether the creature had been smart enough to break the wires on purpose or it had crushed them to uselessness by accident made no difference. The damaged wire had to be replaced or bypassed. "Do we have enough wire to run a fresh line?"

"We barely had enough to reach out through the gate to use the wall for protection. I can patch it in place, but I can't guarantee it will work. The insulation's gone in several places, and I'm afraid the copper is broken somewhere inside the casing where I can't see it."

"Pull as much slack as you can, then see if you can patch it. If that doesn't work, we need another plan." There had to be a solution.

John M. Olsen

Barnstorming

Jackson hadn't seen any creatures since he'd taken out two that had emerged from the trees. Wind pounded at him as always when flying, seeking the openings in his leather cap and jacket, tugging at his goggles each time he turned around to get a view behind him. The smell of the roaring engine was ever-present while flying; a smell that reminded him of the elation he always felt while airborne, despite the constant scent of castor oil used to lubricate the engine.

Between the enemy artillery and his own trickery, he'd led six of the creatures to their doom. Despite the list of successes and efficient use of enemy fire, he still worried over how to proceed. Moreau's machine gun had less than a quarter of its ammunition left. At least the airplane still felt almost as responsive to his touch on the controls as it had before its repairs, despite the gash near his feet.

A slight miscalculation cost him a minute looking for the castle, but he finally spotted it in the remaining moonlight. The Marines were nowhere to be seen at first, but they poured out of the castle unexpectedly at his appearance in the sky, waving their flashlights around.

"Moreau, keep an eye out. They can come at us from above or below. Point as you spot them."

John M. Olsen

His bombardier nodded, and within moments indicated a target below them. A gray mass moved against the darker color of the trees. After the pilot lined up an approach, Moreau made a game of it, popping off a few rounds every time the creature appeared in front of the airplane. Whoever manned the ground machine gun had caught on and used Moreau's shots to great advantage to pepper the creature from the ground.

Even with the extra cover from the machine gun on the ground, the risk grew with time. The flying creatures were the most apparent danger, but there were others. The Central Powers forces wouldn't let his flyby two days in a row stand unchallenged, especially with his attack with the heavy darts. They would investigate, and Jackson's flight path led unavoidably toward the castle. They might not send their full force, but someone was sure to come this way tomorrow to see where the airplane had come from.

The fliers approached a critical choice, and Jackson didn't have the right to make it on his own. He yelled, "We're low on fuel. Stay, or leave?"

Moreau held up a bomb and pointed down as he yelled a reply, "We help them."

Every moment shrank their window of success if he wanted to reach the Aerodrome. If the fuel gauge was right, it would soon be too late to make it home. The men below hadn't signaled for bombs, but he agreed with his partner. He could keep the flying creatures in the air chasing him instead of on the ground tearing the men apart with their claws.

Flashes of gunfire below caught Jackson's attention. The airborne creatures had given him a momentary breather, but something was still going on groundside. The only explanation was that there were more creatures he couldn't see. If they joined the other air creatures, they could force him to choose between abandoning the fight or being overwhelmed as they closed in on all sides, just like they'd done against the Farman MF.11.

No new opponents left the ground to join him in the air. While that was good news for Jackson, the men on the ground had more to deal with. Tracking the beams of their flashlights, he watched as two men went back into the castle, then came back out a short time later. They had to be planning something, but he had no way of telling what their plan was, or if he could help. The only prearranged signals relied on using red lights to mark out a location for dropped bombs, and a signal that the mission was complete. No lights meant no bombs, and the mission was still in progress. He circled, hoping to keep enough pressure off the men on the ground for them to survive.

Curious about why nothing chased him through the dark sky, Jackson banked around and lost altitude for a closer look. The moon approached the horizon, but still provided a little light to spot the creatures when they rose above the trees.

Shots rang out from the ground as a creature swooped through the courtyard, snatched at something on the ground, and flapped into the sky. A small box dangled a few dozen feet below the creature on a cord.

Moreau threw his hands up in the air, then turned to yell to Jackson in frustration. "A detonator and wire!"

If the creatures were smart enough to make off with the detonator for their explosives, he had to take that into account. The only reason they'd left him alone was because they'd seen a better target.

Or they'd found a new way to attack his aircraft.

If that wire got into the airplane's rotor, the plane would go down. "Shoot it down, now!" Jackson had to get close, but not too close. He muttered to himself, "Piece of cake. I fly better than they do."

The creature with the detonator lost no agility as it gained altitude. Didn't they ever get tired? He tried to loop around to get behind it, but the thing could stall, drop, and change directions too quickly. His only advantages were speed and altitude, and he'd lose both if he got into a close fight. After a couple of passes, Jackson saw an opening as the creature dropped into a shallow banking turn. Almost too late, Jackson saw the trap as the wire dangled, not just to the attached detonator, but also hung as a loose strand drifting almost invisibly through the night sky. The creature flung the loose wire up into his path as he roared in for an attack.

Moreau only got a short burst off before Jackson banked hard to the left. The wire slapped against the end of his right wing, tearing a little patch of canvas loose to flap in the wind. It wasn't enough to kill his lift, but if he ended up with enough tears and holes, he'd go down as surely as if his prop got tangled with the wire.

The fight was as much mental as physical. Despite the airflow and cool night air, sweat ran down Jackson's neck. He banked around once more, ready for new tricks from the creature with the dangling wire-turned-whip. If the creature with the wire used the same trick again, he wouldn't be caught unaware.

It swooped down and pulled up from its dive, flapping nearly straight up for a few seconds as Jackson approached. It then flipped over and dove toward an intercept, but where was the wire? Jackson had lost track of it in the darkness. His gut told him something was up, and the creature had a different sort of trick in store for him. Rather than close, Jackson banked hard to the right. The force pressed him down into the seat, spoiling Moreau's shot before he could take it. The creature snatched the falling box and wire out of the air. It had thrown it at the top of its climb, hoping to catch him.

So much for counting on it repeating the same trick. The creature was clever, maybe cleverer than the ones he'd led away from the castle. With that thought lurking in the background, Jackson scanned for the other gargoyles, knowing they had plenty of intelligence to work together.

He had to match them with his flying skills and out-think them to survive. He knew where the machine gun sat, and Moreau still played the game of handing creatures off to the men on the ground when he could. It was time to act instead of react. He took a hard turn and came in for what he hoped looked like another approach like he'd done before, but this time, he lured the nearest creature rather than the other way around, hoping it would make a fatal mistake. As they danced, he pulled it closer to the ground gunner until at last he lined up for Moreau to fire and illuminate it with tracers.

The machine gun on the ground barked in response, several rounds hitting the creature. The creature pulled up in a stall and dropped toward the ground, changing targets. That wasn't the way Moreau wanted it to go, but he had other creatures still to fight, while the gunner on the ground poured bullets into the first target.

Jackson lined up on the one holding the wire, but maintained enough distance to keep the aircraft safe from tangling the prop. Moreau opened up and struck the creature's wing. Amid the concentrated fire, the creature's wing tore, and half the wing broke free. Even over the engine noise, Jackson heard it screech as it headed for the ground.

He muttered an apology for dropping even more creatures into the fight below within the castle grounds and surrounding forest. At least the odds in the sky were more favorable.

After reveling for a moment in his success, it was time to regain a little altitude and evaluate the situation, watching to see what followed him into the sky.

Jackson checked his gauges and was horrified to see his fuel level had dropped. Whether from a leak or losing track of time made no difference. He would never make it home on the remaining fuel in his tank. He and his partner were committed to the fight.

John M. Olsen

Swarming

All thoughts of detonating the TNT the normal way vanished when the wire was stolen by one of the blasted gargoyles. Despite the devastating loss, Jones admired their skill and cunning.

Anderson yelled from several paces back in the direction of their camp, "Incoming on the ground!" He opened up with a volley of five rifle shots, and the squad members pivoted as one to converge and pour rounds into the creature charging through the trees. One wing ended in a stump. The creature froze as a front paw disintegrated at a lucky shot a few feet before it reached Anderson, who reloaded then brought his rifle back up. He stared at the creature with wide eyes, prodding it with his bayonet.

Jones joined him to inspect the unmoving creature. Beside it sat the detonator box with the wires. Sighing with relief, he picked up the box, only to have it fall to pieces in his hands. He dropped the useless parts and rejoined the others, shaking his head.

The coordination of stealing the detonator and wire baffled him. Had one of the ground creatures somehow told the flying gargoyle to take the wire? Did they even understand what the wire or the explosives were? So far, they hadn't seen the crate of TNT as a threat, and Jones was happy to keep it that way. The longer they ignored the TNT, the better chance he had of finding a way to use it.

Most of his men crouched within easy earshot, each watching either the castle or the sky. "I need ideas. How do we detonate the TNT? The creatures inside the castle won't stay upstairs forever."

Miller patted his belt. "A grenade might do it. We have a couple of those brand-new Mills bombs."

"And who gets to pull the pin and run like le crazy man?" asked Davis.

Miller scratched the two-day stubble on his chin. "The timers aren't long enough to pull the pin and run from it. Not with it setting off the TNT. We could tie a rope to the pin if we can somehow stick the grenade to the TNT. Detonate it remotely."

"No," Jones said. "I'll take one of them off your hands in case an opportunity presents itself, but too much can go wrong. Maybe the grenade slips loose, the rope gets snagged, the gargoyles decide to stand on the rope like they did the wires. I'll keep the rope trick in mind as a backup, but we need something better."

Miller gave Jones a look and handed over a grenade. "There aren't a lot of options here that include survival if you use the grenade to set off the TNT."

"Let's call it an insurance policy, Brother Miller." Jones wanted as many paths as he could find between him and a successful mission. If one of them looked a lot like a suicide mission, it just went farther down the list. He accepted the grenade from Miller and stored it at his belt.

Mr. Laurens leaned against a tree, unable to do much more than sit and watch, but he had the energy to speak. "The airplane has bombs, does it not?"

"Yes," Jones confirmed. "A twenty-five pounder Moreau made by hand, and several smaller ones. The other airplane had the biggest load of explosives, but it's gone. Would it work to bomb the castle? Or maybe we could burn it down and set off the TNT that way."

Moore said, "Fire is a bad choice to set off TNT, sir. We need more of a direct hit from an airplane bomb or a grenade if we want to be sure. We have to set it off without warning, so the gargoyles don't have time to respond. How's the airplane going to hit a crate of TNT that's sitting inside the castle?"

Jones considered the various arguments, then remembered he'd seen stars through holes in the roof above the grand staircase inside. "The roof is weak. It's got holes in it you can see through, so it won't take much to make those holes bigger and bring a big chunk of the roof down. Take out part of the roof, and Moreau might be able to run a bomb straight down the middle to hit the TNT. I've heard he's a hot shot with those bombs. He might be good enough to hit a target like that, but we have to give him good markers. How do we get red lamps onto the roof?"

Miller eyed the roof edge. "It's too high to climb without ropes. We either run a rope up the outside with a hook of some sort, or someone sneaks in and all the way up to the roof."

"It's too dangerous to go inside unless we have a viable goal. We're tempting fate with every trip inside, and we risk losing more men." Jones knew their small stockpile of supplies inside and out, and they hadn't packed a grappling hook. "What can we use to—" His eyes fell on the tripod for the machine gun Martinez pointed into the sky.

"Martinez, can you shoot that thing without your tripod?"

"A little longer and it won't matter. All my ammo will be gone soon. The moon's going down, anyway. I won't be able to see a thing up there. If you need it, it's yours."

"Right. Miller, could you use the tripod as a grappling hook?"

Miller's expression was half cringe and half curiosity. "I can throw pretty far, but that's a long throw." He eyed the area in the fading moonlight. "Maybe if I threw from the top of the outside wall, across the courtyard. It's too full of trees to throw from below." He shook his head as he eyeballed the distances. "Doesn't look good, sir. Sorry."

Jones turned back to the castle. "Trees. There are trees in the courtyard next to the castle. The ones on this side aren't very tall, but has anyone been around the back side to see how tall the trees are there? Miller, let's take a quick look around the back of the building. We only have a few minutes of moonlight left." He checked his rifle to assure it had a full magazine and that his service pistol was also ready to go.

A quick walk along the outside edge of the courtyard brought them to the north side of the castle. The trees were, in fact, taller on the shady side. Some had likely been planted there on purpose as part of the courtyard gardens and had grown for over a century unattended. One evergreen in particular towered higher than the crenellated edge of the castle roof, and it stood less than fifteen feet from the wall. Miller gave a thumbs up, and they went back to retrieve supplies, leaving their cumbersome rifles at the camp.

Jones learned halfway up the tree that two grown men in a spindly tree was not a great idea. His ribs flared with pain with every movement as the tree swayed back and forth, causing him to cling to the sappy trunk for safety. "You go up and get a line across to the roof, Miller. I'll wait here so we don't snap this thing in half and kill ourselves."

"Yes, sir." With only Miller proceeding to the top, the tree didn't sway so erratically. Near the top of the tree, Miller leaned forward and back, building swing.

Jones didn't dare yell to ask what he was up to as the tree swayed toward and away from the castle. Even a slight noise of branches against the structure could be enough to draw the flying gargoyles from above or the runners from below. He endured the swinging, then caught on as Miller flung a rope loop over the roof's crenellated edge from only a few feet away. With a few tugs, the rope pulled the treetop snug against the edge of the roof. Miller tied off the rope and gingerly stepped onto the roof before motioning for Jones to follow.

The short hop to the roof was easier on Jones' ribs than a hand-over-hand traversal, so it cut a little effort and time from his climb to the roof. Soon he stood beside Miller, eying the rope and the stones along the edge of the roof. Which ones were perches for the gargoyles? It was impossible to tell in the now-moonless sky, and he didn't dare turn on a flashlight. Not yet.

False dawn wouldn't begin to lighten the sky for another hour.

They each pulled out two flashlights with clear red gel filters over the lights. Miller prowled across the roof to a spot he thought would be over the large entryway and grand staircase on the main floor. He wedged one light between shingles, pointing to the sky, but the second didn't want to stand up straight. A shingle came loose with a tug, and Jones cringed at the noise it made. With the extra shingle, he propped up the light, then glanced over to see Miller finishing his second placement to form the other half of a square that covered a good section of roof centered over the entry inside.

Jones fished out his regular white flashlight and searched the sky for the airplane he could still hear buzzing in circles above the castle. A short burst of tracers gave him its location, and he ran the beam of his light across the airplane several times to get the pilot's attention.

Finally, the pilot responded with a rev of his engine. It was time to clear out and see if this cockeyed long-shot plan had a chance of working.

On his next step, his foot went through the rotted shingles, and he slipped through the hole up to his knee. The sudden movement caused him to tense up, pain shot through his ribs. He stifled a scream clamping his teeth together. Splintered wood clattered into the attic of the castle below him.

Miller grabbed for his arm to help him, but he waved him off. "Too much weight in one place and we both fall through. Get to the tree."

The hole wasn't tight against his ankle, but it bore jagged splinters. He eased his leg out a few inches at a time while drawing his service pistol and flipping off the safety. Noise came from below, but the creature inside couldn't reach high enough to grab him.

Gunfire erupted from the side of the roof. Jones twisted to see Miller lit up by two muzzle flashes. That's all Jones needed to get a rough direction for his target. He rolled to the side on his back, pain shooting through him, and fired three times at the gargoyle descending from the sky. He took aim below its glowing red eyes, hoping to hit a front leg.

More shots rang out as Miller and Jones emptied their pistols to no effect. Without a direct hit on the more delicate parts of a leg, there was no way to stop the beast, short of pulverizing it with gunfire. They didn't have the ammunition for that with just the two pistols.

He didn't care whether the creature stayed on the roof or not, but he had to get to the tree before the airplane looped around for its bombing run. There would be no surviving that.

The creature landed with thud on the rotten wood. Jones scrambled to his feet and limped for the lashed tree. Having seen the speed of the creatures, he had no hope of making it in time. Miller opened up with another volley from his service pistol. The man should have been down the tree by now, but he'd stayed to fight.

Jones held his breath and tucked an elbow tight against his ribs before sprinted the remaining distance to the spindly tree trunk. The gargoyle hadn't chased him. Instead, it stopped, picked up one of the red gel lights, and crushed it before moving to the next one.

It only took a moment to release his own spent magazine, and slap another into his pistol. He screamed profanities at the creature as he poured shot after shot into it, hoping to distract it from its task of removing the roof markers. Miller backed up and hoisted himself over the crenellated roof edge to cling to the tree beside the sergeant.

The gargoyle picked up the third light in a clawed hand and stared into the red glow before biting it in half with a crunch. Jones remembered the grenade at his belt, but held off using it. The blast would remove the signal lights as surely as the creature would.

The roof exploded in a rush of noise mixed with a flash of blinding light and flame.

Bits of wood flew in all directions, pelting Jones. A chunk of wood bounced off his helmet, leaving white sparkles in his vision for a moment. Pain radiated through him from a barrage of small impacts. Debris flew by and slashed his sleeve open, leaving a cut across his right bicep.

A quarter of the roof collapsed into the castle, taking the gargoyle with it into the depths of the building. Jones and Miller clung desperately to the tree for stability. The entire castle shook at the impact of the bomb from above.

Miller laughed and pointed. "Now, *that's* good aim."

Jones didn't understand the humor of the situation, but couldn't help but laugh as well. The trip to the roof had paid off despite several unexpected challenges. "Let's get down from here. You go first, and I'll follow once you're on the ground."

Miller nodded and shimmied down to the side branches just below the edge of the roof.

Glancing up, Jones' eyes grew wide as the gargoyle that had plunged into the castle flapped its wings and rose from the hole in the roof, its red eyes burning like small flames. It had lost an ear and the tip of one wing, but it was still able to fly. The creature spotted Jones clinging to the tree and the ropes that held it against the edge of the roof.

Jones yanked a knife from his belt and cut through the rope in one swift motion.

The tree, now free of its constraints, sprang away from the castle like an overloaded catapult with the weight of two grown men near its top. The tree swung past its upright position and kept going. It bowed as the tip bent farther away from the castle, not slowing. It creaked, then the top quarter of the tree snapped off with the two men still hanging from it more than a dozen feet in the air.

The main trunk, now freed from the top of the tree, whipped up and slammed into the side of the castle with a resounding crash. Stones broke loose at the impact.

Jones and Miller landed in a heap, along with the top of the tree. Jones let out a scream from the added trauma to his busted ribs.

Jones rolled onto his back to stare into the night sky once more as the airplane continued on its evasive path. "You still with me, Miller?" At least his voice still worked.

"Yeah," Miller gasped. "Give me a few seconds."

Jones took a handful of ragged breaths, then struggled to his feet beside Miller, scanning the night sky for the shadowy form he'd seen rise from the ruins of the roof. His night vision still suffered from the flash of the explosion. The light of the flashlights had been only a minor inconvenience by comparison. "Let's get back to the others. It's time for phase two."

"This is the dangerous part," Jones said to his assembled team, as if he and Miller had taken a walk in the park to complete the setup for the new task. "We've sneaked and played defense the whole time. Now it's time to go in with a frontal assault. They'll be waiting for us if they're anywhere near as smart as I think they are."

Mr. Laurens used a dead branch as a crutch to stand, a small miracle of recovery after he'd eaten a handful of packaged food rations and drunk a day's supply of water. "I will join you. Even hands as weak as mine can hold a gun."

Considering the request, Jones realized he was right. They would conquer here or die. If they failed and Mr. Laurens stayed outside, he'd just die a little later than the rest of the team. "Fine. Here's a weapon." He handed over the 1911 pistol from his belt that originally belonged to Lance Corporal Brown then handed over two spare magazines from their supplies as well.

"Very good." Mr. Laurens chambered a round and stuffed the magazines into a pocket.

Miller pulled out another flashlight. "We need lights. Lots of them. Do we have more of the red gel filters?" Several men checked their gear, but no more filters could be found. "Sarge, do we use them as-is and hope the pilot gets the message?"

"We do what we can with what we've got." The telltale buzz of the plane overhead told of the pilot's unseen maneuvers. Jones looked at his watch and swore. "He should be on his way back already. He can't make it home. We're wasting his flight time, and the faster we move, the farther he can fly before he's forced to land. Get those flashlights turned on and move out. Make sure he sees where we're going. The gargoyles will see, too, but that can't be helped. Mr. Laurens, see if you can hit the plane with your light as a signal so he knows we're on the move. Let's go!"

The team sprang into action with their lights out to illuminate their way. Red eyes appeared at a window, then vanished as they approached the main door and entered the castle.

Once inside, Jones discovered the wreckage of the bombing run. A few glowing embers remained on the marble floor, but not enough for a risk of fire. The roof over the entire entry and grand staircase was gone, much of it collapsed onto the stairs and the open floor. Stars sparkled through the huge gaping hole above as they played their lights back and forth.

Miller barked orders to his team, "Set out as many lights as you can and point them at the TNT crate. Run lines of light to it along the floor. It's buried under that pile of broken wood."

Jones added, "Fireteam Two, see if you can get that lumber off it. One minute, tops, and we have to be out of here."

Three gargoyles bounded down the stairs, red eyes aglow. "Make that fifteen second!"

Jones and his team were done with sneaking, and the creatures responded aggressively just as Jones had feared. Two flashlights hit the floor in about the right spot to cast a beam, but others hit and popped, the bulbs ruined from the impact. Shots rang out in the growing darkness.

"Down in front!" The men might be more vulnerable kneeling, but they wouldn't accidentally get shot in the back. More shots followed the creatures as they reached the main floor and plowed through the wooden wreckage to get to the Marines. The muzzle flashes lit up the creatures as they approached. One dropped, frozen as it prepared to leap. The other two sprang, hitting Moore and Davis, knocking them both to the ground.

Davis flung up an arm defensively, and the creature clamped down on it with its powerful jaws. It shook him back and forth by the arm as Davis' scream joined the noise of the melee.

The fireteams swarmed the two creatures. White grabbed a stone leg and levered it away from Moore. "Shoot the leg! Shoot it!" In the wild hand-to-hand combat, it was impossible to shoot from a distance. Someone closed with White and fired several rounds into the ankle near where White held it, finally snapping the foot free. Chips of stone flew, slashing exposed hands and faces. White's hand bled from a large cut from the stone shrapnel. The creature froze where it stood.

Davis continued to scream as more men piled on to attempt the same trick. Jones had a clear path to the creature's head, but that wasn't a useful target for destroying it. Red eyes glared at him. He fired twice into the face from less than a foot away, one shot into each eye. Rock splinters flew, one cutting across Jones' chin and slicing through the strap of his helmet, which fell to the ground.

The creature howled like he'd never heard them howl before. Bits of its shattered eyes fell to the floor, no longer glowing, but the gargoyle still lived. Davis yanked his mangled arm free as the beast opened its mouth to howl, then rolled to the side as the rest of the team wrestled its leg into the air.

A shot rang out from across the room, and the clawed appendage shattered. Mr. Laurens leaned against the wall holding his smoking pistol with both hands, nodding in satisfaction at the precise shot.

With the immediate threats handled, Jones shouted, "Lights. Now!" Whatever lights remained were set out to point at the crate by Mr. Laurens, doing what he could, even while barely standing. Jones kept his flashlight after seeing the other lights were sufficient for the signal.

"Move out. Help the wounded."

Davis said, "Le legs still work." His chewed arm hung at an odd angle as he cradled it. It would take a doctor to put that mangled mess of broken bones back in place, but none poked through the skin. Even while holding his broken arm and wobbling on his feet, Davis insisted on the accent. If it got him moving and outside, that was good enough for Jones.

Anderson grabbed Davis by his still-working arm and aimed him at the door. "This way, hero."

White knelt beside the remains of the wingless gargoyle where Moore lay. "I'll carry him." White hefted his teammate over a shoulder. "Go. I've got him."

Jones counted forms as they left through the open doorway. All accounted for. He followed them, keeping a wary eye out for the remaining airborne gargoyles as his men crossed the courtyard and took cover against the outside of the perimeter wall.

White lay Moore on the ground and knelt beside him, fists clenched.

Jones played his light across White first, noting his eyes pinched closed. Then the light rested on Moore, the red gash across his throat, and his vacant stare. Another life given for the cause. Another member of his squad lost on his watch. Jones had to finish the mission and destroy the source of all their trouble to make his sacrifice mean something. Mourning would come later—if they succeeded.

As a last measure, Jones ran his flashlight along the ground in a line to the castle door over and over, hoping against hope that his message was clear enough for the pilot to see and understand.

Could Jackson and Moreau see the target through the hole in the roof? Did they have bombs left? For that matter, did they have any fuel left? He'd done everything he could and sacrificed more good men on the altar of duty and honor. He had nothing left to give besides his own life. He handed off his best hope to a pilot who could no longer make it home. Brother Miller had asked him once if he prayed, and he'd said he had no use for it. But for the first time in years, Jones prayed.

He prayed for the souls of the men he'd lost, but mostly he prayed for the two men flying above him. If they failed to bring the castle down, his only option would be to use the grenade he carried. Finally, he prayed for the strength to do whatever it took to save his squad.

On Target

Jackson looked over the edge of the fuselage at the ground far below. One of the men aimed a light up into the sky, passing the beam over his airplane. They wanted something again. The bomb on the roof had hit precisely where they'd wanted it, but the result hadn't impressed him. There was a large hole in the roof, and nothing else, not even residual fire. They must have had a goal, but how a hole in the roof helped their cause was beyond him.

He banked the airplane to get a better view of the ground, keeping an eye peeled in the direction of the last gargoyle he'd seen. There were at least a couple more flying creatures still out there lurking in the dark, and they'd coordinated their efforts to attack. His only saving grace was that he knew they were out there, and he knew enough about what they could do to anticipate them most of the time. A single mistake could still doom him and Moreau, but it was his mistake to make.

The men below had their lights on, bouncing across the ground as they ran. That was new. They'd tried for so long to be almost invisible, and now they looked like fireflies in the night as they navigated through the trees far below.

A streak of red eyes flashed by in front of the airplane, so Jackson lined up. A burst of gunfire forced the gargoyle to break off its diving attack, but Moreau reached up and slapped at the feed mechanism to the machine gun.

He yelled from the front seat, working to overcome the engine and wind noise. "No more gun." Jackson couldn't see if the gun was out of ammunition or if it had jammed. In either case, the result was the same. Their only defense against the flying creatures now was his skill at staying ahead of them and out of their way.

The men below had a plan and wanted his help, but Jackson had to wait to see what the plan was, and then discover if they could give him a meaningful signal. If the failure of the last bombing run was any indicator, he might as well fly as far south as he could before being forced to land when he ran out of fuel. He had to do what he could to help them, feeling more a part of *their* team than he ever had among the Aerodrome pilots.

Any chance of making it home in the airplane was long gone now. He might make it as far as halfway, reaching a spot near the French border. He could easily find an empty field or a straight road, but that came after his duty to the team working on the ground. And now, his duty was to figure out what the Marines wanted from him. One last bombing run before he had to leave.

It took two tight banking turns to dodge a creature as it swooped after him, but soon he flew over the castle where the men with lights had gone. Through the hole in the roof, he saw flashes of light. Gunfire. There was no way for him to join in a firefight on the ground, even if Moreau had ammunition and a working gun. The plan had to be something else. From his higher altitude, he cut as tight a turn as he dared, maintaining a view down into the castle as the flashes of gunfire ceased.

Then he saw it. Flashlights laid out to illuminate converging lines on the floor. The lines combined to form a star with a crate at the center. A target on the floor deep within the castle through the hole he'd made in the roof. Those crazy Marines had asked Moreau to blow the roof in, and now they wanted him to drop a bomb down a proverbial chimney. Destroying the roof had only been the first part of their plan all along. The desperation of it amazed him.

Jackson cut the engines for a moment to yell over the noise. "Can you hit that, Moreau? Look inside on the floor!"

"You doubt me? After all we have done? I will hit it." Most would count the speech as bluster. Moreau was good, but was he good enough? It wasn't all up to Moreau. Jackson had to get the flight path right while dodging at least two creatures still winging through the now-moonless night.

A lone flashlight exited the castle, bobbing across the grass under the canopy of trees. A few moments later, the light painted a line back to the castle. The message was loud and clear. It was all up to the pilot and his bombardier now.

Moreau waved a hand, telling Jackson to drop as low as he could go, so Jackson dropped in banking turns, passing over the castle each time around on the way down. One light winked out inside, then another as he watched from above. The Marine with the targeting flashlight still pained a line on the ground to the door of the castle, waving the light like a runway line. The mission was still on, and it wasn't the Marines making the lights go out. It had to be the creatures putting out the lights, ruining the beacon. If the markers vanished, Moreau had only his memory to draw upon while flying over a dark castle with the moon already set. It wasn't just the Marines on the ground who were crazy.

Wasting no more time getting into position, Jackson dropped into a steep dive.

In the front seat, Moreau leaned down, fidgeting with his bombs to enable their fuses.

An approach less than a hundred feet over the top of the roof was the best Jackson could do without risking an impact with a tree or hillside. Moreau signaled full throttle as Jackson lined the airplane up with the dark silhouette of the castle, almost invisible if not for the occasional gleam of flashlights. He jammed the throttle to full, gaining speed.

Just before crossing over the courtyard, Moreau signaled for an Immelmann maneuver. A repeat of the trick he'd pulled during their recent daytime run that now seemed ages ago. There was no point in second-guessing Moreau now. It was all or nothing. He dipped to gain even more speed, skimming a mere thirty feet over the top of the castle, then pulled the stick back to do a half-loop.

Moreau bobbed his head at one second intervals, timing his drop. Red eyes flashed overhead and banked in a hard turn, working to intercept them as the airplane climbed and came out upside down at the top of the half-loop.

Moreau stood in his seat with his head dangling near the top wing. He let loose his large twenty-five-pound bomb, along with his remaining stockpile of smaller bombs, dropping them into the now dark hole in the castle roof. The man had to have the night vision of a jungle cat to see well enough to hit anything, and now he and Moreau were completely unarmed.

Jackson flipped the airplane upright as a shock wave hit from the explosion below, jarring the airplane. The force of the blast far exceeded what Jackson knew the larger bomb could do, even throwing in the smaller bombs for good measure.

The diving gargoyle's red eyes winked out of sight. Afraid it was a new trick, Jackson banked evasively, then leveled out turning south.

A shape tumbled past, its wings outspread but immobile as it rushed to the ground.

Jackson peered behind at the castle. The walls collapsed outward. A giant fireball rose from the interior into the night sky. The entire castle collapsed into rubble.

With the fall of the airborne creatures, his last possible reason to stay vanished. He tapped his fuel gauge and estimated how far he might make it. Nursing the throttle to maximize his range, he yelled to Moreau, "Remember the farm they mentioned on the radio? The one we directed them to?"

Moreau nodded and signaled onward as he watched for any glimmer of landmarks from the ground.

If he was lucky, he could match up three critical events; the approaching pre-dawn light, running out of fuel, and flying over the farm. They'd said something about a pasture. Anything clear and mostly flat would do.

Colonel Dubois would be furious, but oddly, that didn't bother Jackson like it would have on any earlier mission. He checked the throttle once more, hoping for enough fuel to make it to their new destination.

On approach to the pasture, the engine cut out, then sputtered back to life in time to give him just enough lift to clear the trees and reach open ground. Wheels bounced hard, jarring his teeth at the force of the landing. The engine sputtered to a stop at the far end of the pasture away from the farmhouse as its fuel ran dry. The bumpy landing was a joy to Jackson compared to the crash he'd expected if he'd run out of fuel over the forest. "Well, Moreau, I think that'll do. I'll keep watch and make sure this is the right farm if you want to catch a little shut-eye."

"Oui. I look with joy to spreading my coat out on the pasture under the airplane. Shout if you need me."

John M. Olsen

Jackson headed across the field toward the barn and farmhouse. Vehicles sat hidden in the barn, but his report had also warned of the atrocities committed in the farmhouse by the Kaiser's men. "Barn it is, then," he said to himself.

Signs of the Marines' work became immediately clear. The large door was blocked with a cart to prevent entry, and wheel tracks ran from the narrow road into the barn. If they'd intended to hide what they'd done, they needed much more extensive training. At least they'd made it harder to get to their parked armored cars. Their work had succeeded, if only by luck and circumstance. Nobody was out and about in this area, everyone having either been killed or gone into hiding long before.

After several tries, he budged the wagon and opened the door far enough to squeeze through the narrow gap. There they were. Two armored cars with all the supplies the Marines couldn't carry with them. Given his complete lack of supplies in the aircraft, it was a treasure trove. Jackson longed to drive a car through the forest to help the Marines who'd been forced to abandon the vehicles here, but the trees were too thick, and he had no way to predict their path.

A crate of food made Jackson smile. If the Marines had survived the castle and returned, they might have dinner together. Military rations weren't great, but they were far better than going hungry.

Jackson's eyes lit up as he spotted the fuel cans. They'd brought enough to fill the cars back up for the return trip, and then some. The gasoline might not be exactly what they used at the Aerodrome, but it would do. He didn't need much, after all. The American squeezed a fuel can through the door and stacked it on the wagon outside, then followed that with a second can.

Oil for the airplane engine was another matter entirely. The Marines had no reason to stockpile castor oil. He'd rely on the oil already in the airplane and hope it was sufficient. If he ruined the engine, the head mechanic at the Aerodrome would take him to task. Soon he was back at the airplane carrying the cans.

Moreau stirred. "You found fuel? We could fly the rest of the way home." The bombardier scanned the field, which was barely long enough to work as a runway.

"No, I think we should wait for the Marines. If they make it back at all, they'll be here by evening. I'm sure Colonel Dubois has already written us off as another loss. Showing up later than we already are won't change much. There's one thing we can do, though. Sergeant Jones mentioned a family was killed in the farmhouse. They need graves."

"I am feeling better after a quick nap. Perhaps I should start digging while you rest."

"There'll be time for me to rest later. I keep thinking about that family, and I can't rest until they do. I saw shovels in the barn."

"Then we share the task," Moreau said. "Did they leave ammunition behind that will fit my machine gun? I hate to fly defenseless."

"We can dig through the supplies when we're done caring for the family."

Jackson waved from the side of the barn as the Marines trudged into view at sunset, covered in filth and leading two packhorses. Draped across the back of the horses were two bodies, both in Marine uniforms. Missing were the bodies of the two from the downed aircraft that had flown out with Jackson. A Marine held Mr. Laurens upright, and another helped a squad mate whose arm showed red through layers of bandage and a splint.

"Mr. Laurens, you survived!" Others hadn't fared as well. Jackson mourned the loss of Petit and Durland, the aviators who'd gone down in the other airplane.

The spy waved a weary hello as he slumped to sit in the grass beside the path to the farmhouse.

"What about the others?"

Mr. Laurens rested his head in his hands. "We buried them. The sergeant has their identification tags. He only had room to bring his own men back. Bringing the others would have been…difficult."

Jackson recalled the explosion and fireball of the other airplane, gaining a new appreciation for Mr. Laurens' skill at understatement.

Jackson scanned the equipment carried by the team. "What happened to the radio?"

Jones coughed into his hand. "There was what you might call a malfunction. It was broken beyond repair, so we left it behind. The lighter load helped us make better time."

The chuckles from the remaining Marines indicated there was more to the story, but Jackson let it slide. Reporting on the mission had to wait until they could share both their successes and their losses in person with

Colonel Dubois. The fallout would be extensive, he had no doubt.

Calling back to the side of the barn to his bombardier, he said, "Moreau, they're here."

The Frenchman looked up from where he knelt beside the fresh graves of the family he'd helped lay to rest. He'd stayed there holding a shovel and watching over the graves for the past hour, and Jackson had no desire or need to disturb him. Everyone paid their respects differently, and they dealt with the horrors of war in their own way. This mission had contained enough horrors to last a lifetime, yet the war would continue to bring more trials. Of that, he was sure.

"Sergeant Jones, you and your men can get cleaned up in the house."

Jones gave him a side-eye look. "You know what's in there, right? We told you on the radio."

"The family's been buried. Most of the signs of the massacre are gone. Rest and clean up. Moreau and I will lay out the men from the packhorse and gather rations for supper."

Jones gave a weary nod of acceptance. "You heard him, men."

How the men still put one foot in front of the other was a mystery. With the lack of sleep and the miles of hiking, it was a wonder they could still walk.

Soon, Jones reappeared with the grime cleaned from his hands and face. He collapsed onto the wagon that still blocked most of the barn door and grimaced at a hidden pain. "I'm glad you and Moreau made it out with your airplane. It was well beyond your mission parameters to stay as long as you did. You're the only reason we succeeded."

Jackson wasn't about to admit that he'd overstayed by accident after losing track of time. If he'd remembered and watched his fuel properly, would he have left them? There was no way to know. The world was full of what-ifs. You could argue forever what you might have done or not done. The only thing that mattered was what had come to pass.

"Did it work? Did collapsing the castle do everything you hoped?"

"We watched the last gargoyle turn back into stone at sunrise. It dug through the rubble and flames in a frenzy before it froze, but failed to find its home perch in time. We broke the statue into pieces with hammers afterward, just in case. The only chance of anything surviving is if one of them was deep in the basement where we found

Mr. Laurens. If one of them is down there, it has an entire castle collapsed on top of it now."

Jackson noted the nonchalant way Jones referred to the creatures. "You're not here in Europe because of the war, are you? You've done this sort of thing before."

"Sorry, I've said too much. You're asking questions with answers above my pay and rank. Unless…"

"Unless what?"

"You've seen up close how the war is going and what airplanes can do. You kept your cool when things got weird. Your reports were textbook cases of how to describe a bizarre situation with as much detail as possible without sounding like a loon."

"Where are you going with this, Sergeant? It almost sounds like you're working out how to compliment me for not being an idiot." Jackson had heard a similar preface when asked to fly with the Frenchmen at the Aerodrome as a military consultant, so he knew what typically came next.

"You did well. I can either try to convince you that those were large rabid birds and swear you to secrecy forever, or I can offer you a chance to make a difference. Not just in this war we all know is growing. Not just people shooting at people while governments bicker back and forth. What's the chance of convincing you that extra-large eagles took down multiple airplanes?"

Jackson stiffened as he realized this would be one of the most important interviews of his life, and he felt utterly unprepared. "If you mean, can I be trusted to keep my mouth shut, that's not a problem. You saw my reports. Just the facts, and a lot of deniability. The military has beaten that into me. If you mean to ask more than that, I'm listening."

"You have skills. We could use you in Special Unit 13. I can put in a word for you if you're up to the challenge. We've had men transfer in before when they've proven themselves. As we sit now, the least I can do is to get you and Moreau out from under that useless Colonel Dubois. Mr. Laurens, too, if I can convince my chain of command that a foreign advisor is a good person to get to know.

"The short of it is, the world is weirder than you thought it was. We're here to protect ordinary people against the evils that lurk in the shadows. That's not a metaphor. We fight actual evil, and the moral and physical darkness it uses to hide from view. From where I sit, I like that a whole lot better than waiting while others decide which king, president, or congressman deserves to be listened to."

"Sign me up. Or put me on your list. Whatever it is you do. I've already burned through whatever good will I had with Colonel Dubois, so I'm happy to relocate. If the fight is against the darkness, as you say, it's easier to see I'm on the right side."

Jones gave a tired smile tinged with sadness. "Knowing you're on the right side of the fight doesn't help as much as you think it might, but you're right; I have no doubts why I fight or who I fight for." Jones rested a hand on his chest and winced at the movement.

The following morning, Jackson went through his preflight checks on the aircraft. The creatures had done more cosmetic damage to the aircraft, but nothing severe enough to keep him from flying. He didn't remember receiving most of the scrapes and claw marks along the airplane's fuselage and wings, since he'd been so busy dodging. Now it was time to face Colonel Dubois for what was most likely the last time.

Jackson had talked late into the night with Jones and his men, those who hadn't collapsed into an exhausted sleep. Around a small campfire, he'd learned a little of the long history of Special Unit 13 and their role in protecting their nation. Many of the details were fuzzy and described in broad, general terms, of course. He wasn't one of them yet, but the more he learned, the more confident he was with the decision to join them.

He held no illusion as to where he might serve. Anyone in the military family knew that duty called, and people answered, going where they were assigned to solve problems nobody else could handle. The overall parameters fit well with his military discipline.

Finishing his check of the machine, he called out to his partner, "Moreau, are you ready to go?"

"One minute while I feed the ammunition belt into the gun. Your friends gave me enough rounds from the supplies in the cars to keep me from feeling naked as we fly home."

Home. It wouldn't be his home for long. "You know, in the military, home is an odd concept. Sometimes it's where you sleep. Sometimes it's where your support and orders come from. Sometimes it's where you were raised or where your family lives. They're all different, but they're all home in some way." It was time for him to uproot from his most recent home and move on, but he had one last task to handle first.

"Call out when you're done, and let's get this airplane back to the Aerodrome. I can't wait to see the look on Colonel Dubois' face when he sees us."

"You are a strange man, Lance Corporal Jackson. Strange, indeed. I could stand to wait quite a long time before talking to the colonel, but we must. You may be prepared to move on from the Aerodrome, but I am not. It is my chance to excel and to fight for France." He closed the feed mechanism to the gun. "Everything is ready now."

Jackson fired up the aircraft and rumbled across the pasture, gaining speed, then pulling up and dodging between the farmhouse and the barn as he climbed into the sky. Below, the Marines also abandoned the farm, driving the path that had brought them there. He would beat them to the Aerodrome by several hours. Time he would most likely spend standing at attention, reporting to Colonel Dubois, and being reprimanded.

He traversed the series of familiar towns he'd used as markers along his path. Too bad there wasn't enough borrowed fuel to take a less-direct flight back.

Lance Corporal Jackson entered his fourth hour of grilling at the hands of Colonel Dubois. It wasn't going well, because Jackson refused to fill in details on the enemy they'd fought, or why it was so important to blow up an entire castle of possible historical significance. He'd been over the parts about fighting the flying enemy several times, while leaving out the parts about them being gargoyles.

Even spending the extra night in the field had come under the colonel's scrutiny, since it had kept a flying resource out of Colonel Dubois' hands for an additional day.

"Why is it, Lance Corporal, that you feel qualified to advise and help us here at the Aerodrome? You've been evasive. I suspect you have lied to me. You have given me no good reason for many of your actions, yet you expect me to accept what you have done without revealing the details of the mission you shared with those ego-bound Americans."

As Jackson prepared to speak, raised voices came from the secretary's desk outside the office. Jones let himself into the office. "Ah, Colonel Dubois. So good to see you." Jones wore the same uniform from the day before, still spattered with blood and showing dozens of scrapes and cuts from the mission. A large bandage covered his chin, and a scab showed through a cut in his sleeve. "Do you mind if I sit? It's been a long couple of days."

"If you must be so lazy, then do so." The colonel's sour expression fit his words like a well-oiled glove.

"Sorry for my appearance. I haven't had time to locate a clean uniform since our last enemy engagement. I've just come from the telegraph office, and they had a message for you, so I decided to deliver it to you myself out of the goodness of my heart." Jones reached from his seat and placed a sheet of paper on the colonel's desk in easy sight of Jackson.

Scanning down the message from where he stood, Jackson's eyes grew wide as he stood at attention. Of all the places Jackson could be, standing at attention in this room had suddenly gone from the bottom of his list to the top.

Jackson watched the colonel as he read the message, his face going purple with rage. "This is an outrage! I will not tolerate your petty revenge. This Aerodrome is mine!"

Jones leaned back into his chair. "According to your new orders, that's not the case. Feel free to argue with your commanding officer over the change. I'm afraid they weren't keen on the more creative recommendations I shared with you over the radio, so you'll have to make do with your cavalry reassignment. If there's nothing else, I also have orders for the reassignment and transfer of one Lance Corporal James Jackson. Oh, what a coincidence to have him here already. It turns out other organizations have a great need for such a dedicated and skilled man. If there's nothing else, sir, I'll gather him and be on my way."

Colonel Dubois stood with fists planted on his desk, his face twisted in anger. "Get out. Both of you."

Jackson didn't need to be told twice. He was out the door as fast as decorum allowed, working to hold his expression still until he and Jones were outside the building.

"You could have warned me, sir."

"You're right, I could have, but this gave me a chance to watch his reaction and yours at the same time. Life doesn't give me many special moments these days, so I take them where I can get them. We leave as soon as you can pack. We have folks who want to speak to you about the potential of aircraft as they continue to improve. I have a feeling this could be big."

"What about the Aerodrome? If Colonel Dubois is gone, who is coming in? There are a lot of poor choices for his replacement out there that won't make things better."

Jones glanced back at the building they'd left. "I burned up most of my favors and a few borrowed from my chain of command to get the colonel reassigned. The only thing I had left was a recommendation for a field promotion for Sous-Lieutenant Marcel Moreau. He won't be high enough rank yet to take over the whole Aerodrome, but he can play a key role here serving under a new commander. It's good to have friends in key places like this."

Something nagged at Jackson. "You're not taking me out of the air to put me behind a desk, are you? That's why I ended up here in Le Bourget as an adviser in the first place. I love flying, and I hate desks."

Jones shook his head. "No, not many of us have the luxury—or curse—of staying behind a desk for long. We want you where you can do your best work, but I doubt you'll spend all your time in the air. I've put in my recommendation to get you onboard. Don't disappoint me, Jackson. There's a lot to do. Whether in the air or on the ground teaching, we need people like you."

Jackson had never thought seriously about that side of the equation. Someone needed his skills and knowledge and had gone out of their way to bring him into their team. These were the kind of men he could work with and fight beside honorably.

"Looks like Special Unit 13 will feel like home in no time, sir."

Jones clapped him on the shoulder. "I think you'll fit in just fine."

Epilogue

My Dearest Pearl,

Our last mission was a success, just like the one before. During the assignment, I was able to visit an old castle where I learned about interesting features of its architecture. I still don't know when I'll get to Paris, but my hope springs eternal. I drove through an area nearby, but it was too far away to see anything. Maybe my first time there will be when I take you along with me after the war. Just you, me, and the baby. I still don't know if I can be there when the baby is born, but I know you're strong, and you have both your parents and mine to rely on to make sure everything goes well.

I think of you day and night. Everything I do is for you, because I love you more than life itself. When this is over, I want to put talk of war behind me and focus on you and our child. Home and family take on a different meaning out here with the bonds we form in the Marines, but you're my only true love. The only home I want is with you.

I still remember what you told me after that last long kiss at the train station. Nothing in the world can come between us. My job keeps me away for the moment, but this too shall pass, and I fully expect to grow old with you and tell war stories to our many grandchildren as I bounce them on my knee decades from now.

I need to visit a hospital to see an injured Marine tomorrow, so I should get some rest rather than stay up all night hunting for the perfect words to send to you. I'm afraid my words will never be perfect, and the things I write will never match even a fraction of what I feel.

Know that I love you with my whole heart. I will always stand between you and the dark, and I will do what it takes to keep you safe and happy.

All is well, and I hope to finish this tour in Europe in a few months. I'm still working out how to put together that properly romantic letter I keep promising, but my Marine muscles keep getting in the way of my aching, homesick heart. I'm sure you can fix that for me with a kiss when I return home.

Perhaps in my next letter I can tell you more of what I've been up to.

You are my strength and my inspiration in all that I do.

With love, forever and always,

Sgt. George Jones, USMC

The military hospital smelled of antiseptic and pain. Once the doctors had put a fresh bandage around his ribcage and cleaned up his other cuts and scrapes, Jones insisted on being allowed to visit Davis and Mr. Laurens in a large room across the hall. The other squad members had been treated for minor injuries and released, but Davis wore a fresh plaster cast on his arm.

"How long are they keeping you here, Davis?"

"Le doctors haven't told me yet, sir."

Jones glanced at the chart hanging on the end of the bed and couldn't make heads or tails of it, but he'd spoken with someone from the medical team earlier. "It's good to see they were able to get that break set properly. They lectured me for not setting it properly in the field, but here we are. Keep up with the butchered French and they'll kick you out sooner to be done with you."

A French nurse in a spotless white uniform approached with a lunch tray. "Oui, but some of us think it is adorable." Jones wasn't sure, but it sounded like she'd emphasized her accent on her last word.

Davis got a dreamy look on his face, probably due to a mix of morphine and the attention of the nurse who appreciated his quirkiness. He would happily stay in the hospital as long as they let him if that's the sort of attention he got.

"And you, Mr. Laurens? Feel free to correct his French if you're up to it. Let me warn you that it may tax you beyond your abilities. I hear you'll be up and about soon and may be able to escape his tortured grammar."

"Yes, I am doing better. One more day of observation and they will kick me out."

The nurse raised a playful eyebrow. "Release, not kick out. I would never kick you out." She made a couple of notes on each chart, moving with efficiency even as she traded eye contact with both patients.

The reason for her actions dawned on Jones. She wasn't a flirt. Rather than merely treating the physical wounds of her patients, she treated the emotional scars, giving them something to focus on besides the horrific pain and trauma the injured men endured. The hospital was lucky to have her.

Turning back to Mr. Laurens, Jones said, "I've put in a word on your behalf with my chain of command. We could use a good set of eyes out in the wild."

A sly grin crept onto Mr. Laurens' face. "A member of my chain of command and yours have spoken at length. They are familiar with your work. We may be in touch soon. Your assignments are quite interesting. Terrifying as well, but definitely interesting. I would consider working with you in the future."

"I look forward to our next meeting, Mr. Laurens. Davis, I'll see you when they're sick of keeping you here."

Davis gave a salute that failed almost every regulatory test, and Jones stood straight and returned it. He would take a full squad of men like Davis if he could, warts, pranks, and all.

Jones walked to the front desk where he could arrange a ride back to the hotel, grimacing at the pain each time he twisted a little too far.

The hotel room hadn't changed during the mission. Jones didn't even know if they'd assigned it out to someone else while he and his team were away in Belgium destroying gargoyles. It really didn't matter much, but he appreciated the familiarity of being given the same room. The small hearth still sat empty for the summer, with no wood stacked beside it. Bits of ash sat in the back of the hearth from the letters he'd burned a few days earlier. It felt more like an eternity ago.

Jones had sent all the necessary telegrams, informing the families of Lance Corporal William Brown and Lance Corporal Edward Moore of their valiant service and ultimate sacrifice. The cover story of being ambushed by enemy forces was vague enough to be true, if you looked at it sideways and squinted hard enough. It allowed Jones to describe the men as the true heroes they were, stalwart defenders of hearth, home, and country.

Jones asked specifically if he could also send kind words to the families of the other men who'd died on the mission who weren't under his command. Their families deserved to know their brothers, sons, and fathers had died serving with honor in a fight against evil. It was a shame he couldn't clarify what sort of evil they'd fought, but his assignments preserved their ignorance of things nobody should have to worry about.

The chest wrap applied by the doctors itched, and his ribs ached horribly. There was little to do but convalesce and wait for the breaks to heal. He struggled to his feet with a grunt of pain and walked to the box a valet had delivered to his room. It held everything the medical team had rescued from his mangled and stained uniform, including the bundle of letters from the inside breast pocket of his jacket. Picking up the letters, he made his way back to the desk, where he looked over his freshly penned letter to Pearl. He folded the lone sheet of paper of the letter and slid it into an envelope, then carefully wrote out his home address below Pearl's name.

Taking the bundle of letters he'd written during this most recent mission, he sat at the hearth to untie them and spread them out. One by one, he read through the letters, and one by one he set a match to them, watching them burn and become yet another bit of ash in the back of the hearth. Someday she might see his bravery and how he really fought for her, but it would only be at his death. Until then, he'd preserve her innocence as he preserved her safety with his every mission and his every breath.

He would be her unsung hero, giving her a sense of hope borne of the innocence everyone deserved.

Making his slow way back to the desk, he sealed the envelope and gently kissed it, then set it aside to go out in the morning mail.

The End

Bio:

John M. Olsen edits and writes speculative fiction across multiple genres and loves stories about ordinary people stepping up to do extraordinary things. His short stories have appeared in dozens of anthologies. He hopes to entertain and inspire others as he passes on a passion for reading to the next generation.

He loves to create and fix things through editing and writing both short stories and novels, and also when working in his secret lair equipped with dangerous power tools. In all cases, he applies engineering principles and processes to the task at hand, often in unpredictable ways.

He lives in Utah with his lovely wife and a variable number of mostly grown children and a constantly changing subset of extended family and pet

If you enjoyed High Hopes by John M. Olsen, then check out these other JTF-13 titles.

JTF-13 Origins Anthology

Legacy Cover art ISBN 1951768337

John M. Olsen

Widowmakers

Legacy Cover art ISBN 1951768329

Sea Serpent

ISBN 1951768361

John M. Olsen

Witch Hunt

ISBN: 9781951768409

www.ingramcontent.com/pod-product-compliance
Lightning Source LLC
Chambersburg PA
CBHW060922190726
48286CB00002B/603